"What you know about men could fit on a stamp."

"I know all I want to about *you*!" Christie snapped.

"Do you now?" Logan said with lazy mockery as his hand caught her chin and turned her face toward him. "Tell me what I'm thinking now."

Their eyes met, and Christie knew precisely what he was thinking. Her whole body pulsed with awareness. There was still that sexual magnetism between them. She remembered all too vividly how their bodies fitted together—and how far apart their minds had been. She was afraid. She didn't want to risk another try.

Logan's hand dropped, and his face changed. "If you want to see Kit, you'll see him when I'm around to make sure you don't try to make off with him."

"The way *you* did!" she snapped.

"Exactly!

Books by Charlotte Lamb

A VIOLATION

HARLEQUIN PRESENTS

HARLEQUIN ROMANCES

These books may be available at your local bookseller.

For a list of all titles currently available,
send your name and address to:

Harlequin Reader Service
P.O. Box 52040, Phoenix, AZ 85072-2040
Canadian address: P.O. Box 2800, Postal Station A,
5170 Yonge St., Willowdale, Ont. M2N 5T5

CHARLOTTE LAMB

a naked flame

Harlequin Books

TORONTO • NEW YORK • LONDON
AMSTERDAM • PARIS • SYDNEY • HAMBURG
STOCKHOLM • ATHENS • TOKYO • MILAN

Harlequin Presents first edition December 1984
ISBN 0-373-10747-1

Original hardcover edition published in 1984
by Mills & Boon Limited

CHAPTER ONE

ZIGGY was whistling through his teeth as he drove along the Promenade des Anglais. Christie recognised the tune at once; it was the theme music for her latest film. Ziggy had composed it, and it had that special quality which his music always had, and which made him highly demanded by the film world: haunting, poignant and yet memorable. When the film was released Christie was certain half the world would be whistling it.

Ziggy turned to smile at her, and stopped whistling. 'Will you marry me?' It was a light question and one he had asked many times before in the same light tone.

Christie laughed. 'Ask me tomorrow.' That was how she always answered him, and he had always smiled and said: 'I will, don't worry.'

Tonight, though, he said gently: 'There are no more tomorrows, Christie. Give me my answer now, and if it's no, this time it's final.'

She was taken aback and stared at him uncertainly, a hundred different reactions flashing through her. Ziggy looked unfamiliar to her, he was serious, and that was rare enough to startle her into attention. Ziggy had always made her laugh, even when he proposed. She had never seen him fight to get attention, the way most people did in the film world—yet he always got it, people found him funny, they started to smile as soon as they saw him. Oddly, he didn't have a comic face—he was distinctly good-looking, in a lazy, casual fashion, fair-skinned, with sunny blond hair and blue eyes and a long, slim body which moved with lounging grace. His voice drawled, blurring words, he often sounded sleepy and he found other people as amusing as they found him, his blue eyes smiled all the time.

Christie did not know what to say to him now. She tried to change his mood, hurriedly laughing. 'Is this goodbye, Ziggy? You wouldn't break my heart, would you? You know I couldn't say goodbye to you.' She said the words teasingly, lightly, watching for his usual wry smile.

'I mean it, Christie,' he said, though, and he wasn't smiling.

'Oh,' she said, suddenly cold. She felt like crying, she was aggrieved because Ziggy was changing the rules of their game without warning. For four years they had been friends, always seen around together at first nights and parties, spending days on the beach at Malibu together in between working, and she would be lost without Ziggy, but she knew she wasn't in love with him. As a man he lacked some vital ingredient. Perhaps he was too civilised? Women always liked him, but they didn't lose their heads over him. Christie hadn't lost her head, either, but she loved Ziggy, he had become an essential part of her life. She couldn't bear to lose him, it would be like losing her right arm.

'I'd rather have it straight,' Ziggy said. 'If I'm wasting my time, say so. Can't you love me, Christie?' He was still driving along the wide straight road along the bay, palm trees on either side, the pavements thronged with holidaymakers who, like themselves, had just had dinner and were taking a stroll, many of them with some vague hope of spotting a celebrity. The Cannes Film Festival was a magnet for all sorts of people: film buffs, ambitious young actors, curvy starlets who hadn't yet made it into a film, producers pushing for a chance to show how good they were, men hoping to pick up one of the pretty starlets, photographers on the prowl for a famous face to snap.

Both Christie and Ziggy were wearing dark glasses and had the smoky windows of the car closed, while the top was rolled back to let the warm sea breeze cool their faces. They didn't want to be recognised.

'I *do* love you,' Christie said vehemently, looking at him. 'But . . .'

'But what? You're worried how Kit will take it?'

'Kit loves you, too, you know that.' Her five-year-old son thought Ziggy was great fun, when the two of them were together they giggled all the time as though they were the same age. Ziggy had that rare adult ability to operate on a child's eye level mentally without talking down or condescending. When he was with Kit he simply shed thirty years.

'I love Kit,' Ziggy said quietly. 'He's a great kid.' He was driving with his eyes on the crowded road ahead. Nice was a car-driver's nightmare; there was never anywhere to park and the traffic jammed up every road. 'We're together all the time anyway, Christie—getting married would only

mean that we would belong together openly. I want
a family. I want you for my wife and Kit for my son.
I want to live with you and Kit, not come and go.'

'Kit has a father,' Christie said in a flat voice.

There was a brief silence, then Ziggy asked: 'Is
he the reason why you won't marry me?'

'In one sense,' she admitted. 'I've been married
and I blew it, and I don't want to make the same
mistakes again.' She smiled wryly. 'I always try to
learn from my mistakes.' Her first marriage had
been an indelible lesson. it had taught her a lot
about herself and about men, and she had made
up her mind that she was never going to take such
risks again. Falling in love made you vulnerable, it
made you easy to hurt, you can't be hurt if you
don't care. The last thing she wanted to do was fall
in love with some man who would try to take over
her life.

She had had that once, but now she was her
own mistress, she ran her own life and nobody
told her what to do. That was the way she wanted
it. Ziggy wasn't the dictatorial type, of course; he
was tolerant and permissive and charming in his
lazy sunny way, but then she wasn't married to
him. You could never be sure of men; once put
yourself into their power and something changed
in them. They started taking themselves too
seriously, they began making demands. They
reverted to type, she thought, her mouth wry.

Ziggy had taken the road to Monte Carlo. Far
below them on the right the sea glittered, in
moonlight, but the moon was a pale ghost by
comparison to the neon lights along the Côte
d'Azur, they outshone every planet in the galaxy.

'I'm not Logan Gray, and you're not eighteen any more,' said Ziggy. 'How long have you known me? Four, five years? Don't you know me well enough to believe I wouldn't give you the same treatment he did? Why do you think I've waited so patiently? I knew what you'd been through with him. I wanted to give you time to learn to trust me. Don't confuse the way he was with the way all men are.' He looked round at her and smiled, his hair almost white in the moonlight. They had halted at traffic lights; Christie stared fixedly at the tiny red glow. Red for danger, she thought. Marriage was dangerous, she had learned that very young. Far too young—she should have waited; people shouldn't be allowed to fall in love until they were old enough to handle it, you can pick the wrong person and get caught in a nightmare. The lights changed, became amber and then green, and Ziggy sat watching her as she watched the lights. A car behind them hooted in the terse, impatient French way and others joined in, their horns blaring.

Ziggy said something very rude in French and drove on, while Christie started to laugh helplessly. 'Why on earth did you pick a time like this to propose?' she asked, spluttering. 'While you're driving on roads like this . . .'

'I wanted to make sure I had to keep my hands to myself,' said Ziggy with self-deriding amusement. 'I wasn't going to try to rush you off your feet, I know how disastrous that would be. I wanted to keep a cool head, give you a chance to think. It seemed a good idea; get you in a car where you couldn't walk away from me or change the subject, but make sure I was busy using my hands in ways that wouldn't upset you.'

'Oh, Ziggy, you fool!' she said, laughing, then sighed, biting her lip and watching the coastal road unwinding ahead of them, the tail lights of other cars in constant procession. It looked as though the whole world was going to Monte tonight.

'I can't decide now, on the spur of the moment, Ziggy. I'm not in love with you, you see . . .'

'I know, but you said you love me.'

'I do.'

'And you enjoy being with me.'

'Of course I do.'

'We've spent so much time together we might just as well have been married!'

'That's true, but . . . Ziggy, are you in love with me?'

He didn't answer for a moment and when she looked at him his profile was tight in lines of irony. 'You would ask that,' he said lightly. 'Just like a woman—go straight for the jugular!'

'Oh, Ziggy,' she said miserably. 'I don't think I'll ever fall in love again, not like that, not for real. When you love like that you put yourself in someone else's power, you're helpless, it only means getting hurt.'

'Now she tells me!' he sighed. 'You're a little late with that information, Christie. Four years too late, to be precise. I fell in love with you on sight.'

'How can I marry you knowing I'll never . . . you wouldn't be happy, Ziggy, I love you too much to do that to you.' The wind whipped her

hair sideways and it touched his face. Ziggy put a
hand to it, one finger brushing the long silvery
strand. Her hair was several shades lighter than his
and very fine; one separate hair twined around his
finger in a filigree ring, and she watched it with a
sort of shock, as though it bound her to him. Then
it uncoiled and they were separated again, and she
said blankly: 'I'm sorry, Ziggy.'

'I've never been a great romantic,' Ziggy told
her. 'I'm not expecting you to fall in love with me,
I'm happy to settle for good old everyday love; it
wears well and you can rely on it. You and me and
Kit—wouldn't we make a good team?' He slowed
as they came in sight of the casino. 'If you still
need to sleep on it, tell me tomorrow, then. For
tonight we'll see how lucky I am at roulette.'

As they went into the Casino a few minutes later
he was laughing and talking in that light, casual,
lazy voice, and Christie almost wondered if she
had imagined the serious look in his blue eyes a
few minutes earlier. Ziggy was back to normal and
she was deeply relieved; it was like seeing a long-
lost friend again, yet she would never be able to
forget the look he had worn in the car. Her idea of
Ziggy had altered. Many people meeting him for
the first time were taken aback because his
personality did not seem to fit the haunting music
he composed; Christie felt that for the first time
she had glimpsed that man, the man who could
twist the heartstrings with his music, and it left her
confused.

The roulette table was crowded; they watched
for a while without placing a bet. Christie found
gambling boring and was only here because Ziggy

had been eager to visit the Casino at Monte Carlo. He had been born and had grown up in Las Vegas, and had begun his career there, playing the piano in a bar at the age of fifteen. He didn't gamble heavily, but he loved the atmosphere in casinos; it made him nostalgic for home. His parents still lived in Vegas and Ziggy went home quite often. He liked the night life and the glitter and the excitement. Country life made him restless, almost nervous; he couldn't wait to get back to a city. Christie could understand how he felt; she was the same about theatres. When she saw neon lights she felt her nerves prickle with excitement, she would never feel quite the same about cinemas. When you were making a film you had no audience out in the dark breathing and watching you, willing you to project to them; all too often the film crew were bored to death by the time you had got to the fifth take, they wanted to wrap it up and get out for a drink, they'd watched you rehearse and fumble and have your make-up touched up, they were more interested in their cameras or sound equipment than they were in the actors. Christie had made three films now. She was turning down offers while her London agent looked for theatre work for her. He thought she was crazy, of course; but then he thought all actors were crazy. It went with the job. You had to be nuts to want to do it.

Ziggy leaned over to place a bet. '*Rien ne va plus*,' the croupier droned, looking around the table, the wheel spun and everyone watched as the ball dropped into the six. Ziggy grinned broadly as the rake pushed his winnings towards him.

'Maybe my luck's changing!' He settled down to bet steadily and Christie stood next to him, ignoring the glances and curious stares they were getting. Ziggy's face wasn't that well known, but her films had been very successful and highly publicised; her face was only too recognisable. She wasn't the only one around the table who was famous, though; she saw a number of faces she knew, among them Carol Heaven and her latest escort, a muscled young man in a smooth white evening suit who kept giving Christie a smile that flashed on and off like the beam from a lighthouse. When Carol wasn't looking, he smiled. When Carol was watching, he didn't. While she gambled Carol kept one scarlet-taloned hand on his sleeve; she wasn't letting him out of her sight, and Christie really couldn't blame her for that wary suspicion. Given half a chance he would stray to more interesting prospects. Poor Carol, Christie thought, turning away.

'I'm going to get another drink,' she said to Ziggy, who was too absorbed in his gambling to do more than nod and say: 'Okay, honey.'

Christie wandered out of the opulent room. She didn't get another drink, she went to the powder room and looked at herself in the mirror while she renewed her lipstick. She hadn't let herself think about Ziggy's proposal while they were at the roulette table, she was putting off the moment when she had to decide. What would Ziggy do if she turned him down? Would he keep his word and vanish? She would miss him. So would Kit. He had become part of their lives. But how could she marry him?

She sighed and left the room. Someone was leaning against the wall. He straightened as she appeared, smiling, squaring his broad shoulders and trying to look sexy at the same time. Christie had trouble suppressing a giggle.

'Hi,' he drawled in a very poor imitation of a Texan accent. 'How're you, honey?'

'Carol will be looking for you,' Christie said wickedly. 'Momma will spank!'

He went a little red. 'She's only got eyes for the table, she won't miss me for a while,' he said, letting his round blue eyes wander over her. 'That's a hell of a sexy dress, honey.' The way he was staring made her feel he could see what was under the clinging blue silk sheath which was cut on a very simple line; high-waisted with the straight skirt beginning from just beneath her breasts and falling almost to her feet. The neckline was rounded, deep; a sapphire pendant hung around her throat, the round stone set in a cluster of tiny diamonds, as she walked the jewel swung heavily between her half-exposed breasts. He watched it, hypnotised.

'It's hot in here, why don't we go for a cool drive? My car's in the car park.' He put his arm around her waist and Christie pushed him away.

'Keep your hands to yourself!'

Several of the liveried servants were watching them and he knew it, his flush deepened and he scowled. 'Come on, you're not so hard to get, so don't try to kid me. I'll show you a better time than Ziggy Molyneaux ever did . . .'

'Drop dead.' Christie walked back towards the gaming rooms, and he pursued her.

'No broad walks out on me,' he muttered, grabbing her arm.

She tried to pull free. 'Let go of me, you creep!'

'What the hell's going on?' Ziggy almost flung himself across the space between himself and their struggling figures and knocked the other man away from Christie. As he tumbled backwards there was a crash as a large porcelain bowl was knocked over, then the casino security men were all round them. In the struggle Christie's dress had been slightly torn; the silk neckline had ripped downwards. She put her hand over it but too late—a flash bulb was already exploding.

'Hey!' Ziggy said furiously.

The security men chased the photographer, but he vanished into the night. Carol Heaven's escort picked himself up, blood on his lip. He was babbling threats. The security men grimly shepherded all three of them towards the private offices. Carol Heaven had already spotted what was going on, attracted by the shouting and the crashes. Tottering on stiltlike high heels, she brought up the rear, demanding in an ear-splitting voice to be told what was happening.

'Oh, shut up,' her escort muttered under his breath, and she gasped, mouth wide open in a scarlet gash. Carol had made her name in musicals. She couldn't sing; but when she shouted she drowned the music and made people laugh so much they didn't care that her voice was as rough as a cheese-grater and she was totally tone deaf.

She gave a pretty fair demonstration of her musical talents for the next twenty minutes. Christie and Ziggy barely said a word, but Carol made up for that. She accused Christie of trying to steal her young man, she described her in terms which would have made a sailor blush, she yelled and swore and even tried to use her long nails. It was embarrassing; the men all looked the other way. Carol was a good twenty years older than Christie; a full-breasted, narrow-hipped woman with hair tinted with henna and electric black eyes that flashed violently.

Christie was weary by the time they left the Casino. She didn't say a word as Ziggy drove back to Cap d'Antibes. It was nearly one in the morning, but the roads were still as crowded, the people still wandered along the pavements in Nice and old Antibes. The lights flashed, the bars were full, the night was young yet for many of the pleasure-seeekers.

'I don't even know his name,' she said to Ziggy. 'I'd never even spoken to him before. I sometimes think I live in a world of lunatics.'

Ziggy grimaced. 'Looking the way you do, can you be surprised when men try it on?' He took one hand off the wheel and looked wryly at his knuckles. 'I've grazed them. I hit him too hard.'

'He deserved it.' Christie wasn't wasting sympathy on that guy.

'No,' said Ziggy. 'I hit him hard because I saw him doing what I've wanted to do for years—just grab you. It's that old male instinct.'

'It makes me sick!' Christie said with force, and saw Ziggy wince. She regretted the tone she had used, but that was how she felt, what was the point of hiding it? When a man tried to use force on her she felt something snap inside her head; she was so angry she shook with it.

As they drove through Cap d'Antibes itself the roads were quieter, there were few people on foot, although many of the villas were still brightly lit and from behind high stone walls you could hear the voices and laughter of people having a party around a pool. Christie was staying in a villa Ziggy had rented for the month; she had brought Kit and his nurse with her and Ziggy's sister and her husband were there, too. The house was huge, there was room for twenty people.

When they had parked the car in the garage at the side of the villa they walked through the shadowy garden. The cicadas chirped among the cypress trees, there was a ceaseless hum from the building housing the electronic gadgets which kept the pool clean, but it was otherwise peaceful compared to the racket in Nice. The moon carved strange shapes in the light and shade of the garden; the pine trees etched black outlines on the grass and there was a scent of flowers. There was a ten-foot-high hedge of cypress surrounding the estate, enclosing them and protecting them from the world outside.

Ziggy paused before they reached the stone steps into the villa. He turned his face up to the moonlit sky and sighed. 'You're not a gambler, are you?'

'No.'

'I am. I sometimes wish I wasn't.'

Christie was puzzled, frowning. 'Did you lose a fortune at the tables tonight, Ziggy?'

'No, I won at the tables,' he said drily, and waved her up the steps into the villa.

The maid had gone home; she worked there

during the day and lived somewhere in Juan-les-Pins. If she cooked dinner for them she had to be given overtime money, but most evenings they went out to dinner. They were in the South of France for the Cannes Film Festival because Christie's latest film had been entered, the film for which Ziggy had written the music. The producer and director were there, too, and they had all spent some time together; dining with important people or just floating from party to party in a group. They were there to influence people and be around to publicise the film, but during the day they had time to swim in the villa pool and sunbathe in the garden under the pine trees.

The sitting-room of the villa was enormous; square and high-ceilinged with windows on three sides, a cool tiled floor spread here and there with rugs and white-painted walls hung with sketches and watercolours. At night the small green lizards which inhabited the garden scuttled down the thick stone walls and hung upside down to peer into the room through the windows; their bulging eyes blinking every now and then as though incredulous of what they saw.

Ziggy took off his jacket and dropped it on a chair, loosened his bow tie and yawned. 'How about a nightcap?'

'No, I think I'll go to bed.' Christie was still upset over the fracas at the Casino; it had all been so pointless and sordid, but she had a sinking feeling that the photographer would sell his picture to *Nice-Matin*, the local paper, and such a story wasn't the sort of publicity they wanted for the film. She frowned, fingering her torn dress, hoping the picture wouldn't come out or that none of the papers would use it.

Ziggy studied her face. 'Stop worrying, it wasn't your fault that that oaf was drunk and had an ego problem.'

'Maybe not, but if that picture gets into the papers . . .'

'Even if it does, it will all blow over in a few days! It's hardly the end of the world. A little set-to in a Casino? Come on, where's your sense of proportion?'

She smiled under his teasing, relaxing. 'You're right. It was very silly, wasn't it? Oh, I'm just tired, I suppose.'

'You need some sleep—you'll feel fine in the morning. I'm going to have a drink to help me unwind, I'll stay up for a while.'

'Okay, goodnight, Ziggy,' she said, and walked very quietly across the marble-floored hall to the stairs. She did not want to wake Kit. Before she went into her own room she tiptoed into Kit's and found him fast asleep but with his covers kicked off. Christie bent over him as she tucked the sheet around him. He was a thin, restless little boy with energy to burn. She kissed the dark blur of his hair; he had his father's colouring, not Christie's fair skin and hair. His bed was crowded with toys; a rather battered teddy bear and a metallic robot occupied the pillow beside his head. She removed the robot and several toy cars, leaving the teddy in his usual place. Kit didn't wake up, he was sprawled across the bed, his slight limbs heavy with sleep, his face flushed. Christie's heart moved with painful tenderness as she watched him. He

was the one good thing that had come out of her
marriage; which was ironic, because she had not
wanted to have Logan's child; in a sense it was Kit
who had ended her marriage, and before he was
born she had bitterly resented him, she had been
prepared to hate him. Then she had held him in
her arms on the day he was born, Kit had opened
dark blue eyes and Christie had felt the clutch of
love in her stomach. Nobody warned you about
the dangers of loving; you had to find out for
yourself, and she had sat holding the soft, warm
little body feeling confused and guilty and totally
insecure. Kit's arrival in her life had upset all her
plans and at the same time given her life new
meaning; it was bewildering, Christie had had no
idea how to cope with all the new sensations
rushing through her, she had laughed and cried in
the ward until one of the nurses took Kit from her
and gave her a sedative, staring at her clinically as
though afraid she had gone right round the bend.
In a strange sense, that was just what she had
done—she had gone round a new corner in her life
and was facing in another direction altogether, one
she had not expected. Until that moment she had
only planned for herself. Now she would be
planning for Kit, too.

He stirred, turning over, and Christie held her
breath until he was breathing regularly again. She
crept out and went to her own room next door.
The shutters were closed but the air was heavy
with fragrance, a bowl of roses stood on a table in
one corner. Christie undressed wearily. The floor-
length mirror set in the fitted wardrobes reflected
her slender body; skin a pale gold, firm and

rounded like a peach, a few fine hairs visible on her arms—she glanced at it without interest, too familiar with her own image to linger. That was another reason why she preferred the theatre to the cinema; she hated close-ups, when the camera zoomed in on her she felt naked in front of it, it picked up every detail, the fullness of her lower lip, the tiniest imperfection on the skin, blue shadows on her lids. You couldn't hide from the camera; it sought out your weaknesses and magnified them. When you acted on a stage you could use a mask, you could assume another persona, but on a screen you were visibly yourself, there was no hiding place.

She didn't wake up until gone ten; it was a Sunday and they had no engagements, they could spend the whole day lounging around relaxing. Kit and his nanny were eating breakfast when Christie appeared, casually dressed in white shorts and a blue sun top which tied at the midriff in a big bow. She had slept deeply and felt terrific. She kissed Kit before she sat down at the table on the patio outside the house.

'Is the coffee hot?'

'I just made it,' said Janet, pouring her a cup. She was a short, thin girl with a placid face and a very soft voice; she had more patience than Christie did, however naughty Kit was she never lost her temper. Firm and steady, she simply went on saying: 'No, don't do that, Kit, if you break all your toys what are you going to play with tomorrow?' As well as his father's colouring, Kit had inherited his restless energy and sudden tempers. He was intensely interested in how things worked, but that usually meant that he took his toys to pieces to find out what made them tick and then became angry when he couldn't put them together again and get them back into working order. Their home was littered with broken toys. Janet had small, deft fingers; she mended those she could, and she answered all Kit's endless questions when Christie wasn't there. Kit didn't take anything for granted. Christie sometimes wished he would. It was exhausting to face a battery of questions, it was an education for her too, because when Kit demanded: 'What makes electric lights work?' or 'Why are all the trees green?' she would have to go to encyclopaedias to find out the answers to questions she had never asked herself.

Kit had done more than that for her—he had given her a hindsight understanding of his father that she had never had when she lived with Logan, but she had not found out why Logan was the way he was because she had not felt about him the way she did about her son. Kit made her feel protective and tender. Logan had frightened her.

'Can we swim before lunch?' asked Kit as she ate a croissant.

'Later, I want to sunbathe first.' Christie leaned back, staring at the pine tree which grew close to the house, gently oozing a glistening golden resin in the sunshine; tiny beads dropped on to the table and formed little mounds. Kit put out a finger and flattened one.

'It's sticky,' he announced. 'What is it? It looks like thick honey.'

'It's resin from the tree,' Christie told him.

'What's resin?' he asked at once, his thin brown face interested.

She looked helplessly at Janet, who laughed. 'There he goes again,' Christie sighed with wry amusement. 'Maybe we shouldn't answer; then he wouldn't come back with yet another question.'

'I like to know,' said Kit.

'He likes to know,' Janet repeated teasingly, and it made sense. There was so much to know about the world and Kit was in a hurry to find out everything he could, he was consumed with curiosity.

Ziggy's sister appeared at the sliding door leading into the villa; she was wearing a white bikini and over it a silk wrap splashed with orange and green tropical flowers. She halted, blinking in the brilliant sunlight, and slipped on some sunglasses, wincing.

'That sun's too bright.' She padded to the table and sat down, giving them all a weary smile. 'I didn't sleep a wink; it's too quiet here, and I can't sleep with the windows closed all night, but if I open them the mosquitoes get in and eat me alive.' She picked up the coffee pot. 'Is this drinkable? Oh, good. No, Kit dear, I won't have any food.' She shuddered, waving away the woven basket of croissants and rolls. 'Just some strong black coffee.'

'Yeuk!' Kit winced, and Erica laughed, ruffling his hair. Christie watched them, smiling; Erica was a singer who had never quite made it to top billing but who managed to live very comfortably. She took a relaxed attitude to her career, in many ways she was very like her brother, but her husband,

Johnny, was ambitious for her and often grew
impatient because Erica didn't take her work
seriously. They had no children. Erica was as fond
of Kit as Ziggy was, but she cheerfully admitted
that she didn't want any children of her own. She
wasn't, she said, maternal.

'So, what are we going to do today?' she asked
Christie, who shrugged.

'Nothing, preferably.'

Erica lifted her coffee cup in a salute. 'I'll drink
to that.' She looked round at the sound of voices.
'Here they come—isn't that just like a man? Last
to bed, last up, making sure all the work's been
done before they show their faces.'

'Insults,' grinned Johnny, kissing her. 'That's all
I get from you—insults. I'm ravenous, what is
there to eat?'

Christie watched the cypress hedge blowing in
the warm summer breeze; the silky green sheen of
it moving like the sway of waterweed in a river.
Today she had to give Ziggy his answer; and she
didn't know what to tell him. She needed more
time to think, she must make sure she wasn't left
alone with him. She avoided the glance he gave
her, although she was aware of it, and wondered
how she could go on avoiding him for the rest of
the day.

It was easier than she had feared. None of the
party felt much like going into Antibes; they spent
the whole day lounging in the garden by the pool,
occasionally taking a swim, sunbathing on padded
loungers afterwards and reading the books they
had brought with them. Kit played with his toys or
lay on his stomach watching the lizards running up

and down the walls or the enormous blue and gold dragonflies; their wings of filmy lapis lazuli, floating and darting across the pool. Kit had an early supper and before he went to bed Ziggy played Scrabble with him. Erica watched them, smiling, 'Ziggy loves him, you know,' she said to Christie pointedly, and Christie nodded and said she knew Ziggy did, then she carried Kit to bed before Erica could start dropping even broader hints. Erica was on her brother's side, of course, what else could one expect?

Kit fell asleep almost at once and Christie went into her own room and leaned on the sill, staring at the moon, her face troubled. Was she being selfish in wanting Ziggy around without intending to marry him?

From Ziggy's point of view, of course she was, but she felt angry with him for wanting to change their comfortable relationship. Why couldn't he be happy the way things were? She was. She knew she would never fall in love again. All that love had done for her was make her close to suicidal. Looking back on her marriage she saw only the blackness and harshness of pain. Logan had put out the sun and left her in a dark world. She had struggled out of that darkness and she never wanted to go back into it.

Ziggy tapped on the door. 'Christie? Aren't you coming down to dinner?'

The door was bolted. 'Sorry, I'm in bed with a migraine,' she whispered in a weak voice.

There was a silence, then Ziggy said drily: 'You act better on screen, darling.' He didn't argue, though, she heard him walking away, and when he had gone she undressed and went to bed, but she didn't sleep. She felt worried and angry; she felt guilty because Ziggy cared so much and she was fond enough of him to wish he would fall out of love with her and be happy just to be friends; she would miss him if he wasn't there any more, so would Kit. Ziggy was a wonderful friend. Why couldn't he stay just that?

The following day she had a lunch engagement in Cannes. She was up early, breakfasting with Kit and Janet, when the maid arrived with the morning newspapers. Christie skimmed through them for news of the Film Festival. *Nice-Matin,* of course, was full of it; pictures and stories on every page, during the Film Festival the whole world came to the South of France and the local paper was only too happy to celebrate the fact. She turned a page and groaned as her eye fell on her own face.

'What's wrong?' asked Janet, wiping chocolate from around Kit's mouth.

'Nothing,' Christie said grimly, staring at the grey photograph. It was slightly blurred, but there was no difficulty in distinguishing faces. There was Ziggy looking uncharacteristically violent, scowling, the other man sprawling backwards with a surprised expression, herself clutching her torn dress and wide-eyed with shock. She read the story, wincing; typically French, it implied a love triangle, jealous rage, herself caught between two lovers. 'Oh, damn,' she muttered.

'Mummy said damn,' Kit pointed out to his nanny.

'If you've finished your breakfast we'll go and swim, shall we, Kit?' Janet suggested tactfully.

'Why did you say damn, Mummy?' Kit asked as Janet hustled him away from the table. 'Why did she? Why?' His voice died away inside the villa and Christie picked up one of the other papers, an English one. That had the picture, too, and a shorter story, rather more discreet than the one in *Nice-Matin*. It hinted, where the French story plainly stated, that she was having an affair with both men.

Ziggy came out on to the terrace, freshly showered, his face smoothly shaven. He gave Christie a wry smile. 'Migraine gone?' It was a mocking question, he hadn't believed she had a migraine last night. She didn't answer, she simply held out *Nice-Matin*. Ziggy glanced at the page, sat down abruptly and stared at it, grimacing. 'Hell,' he said through his teeth.

Christie drank some black coffee, she wasn't hungry although she had skipped dinner last night. She was usually on a pretty strict diet. Her metabolism burned up her food at a terrific rate, she worked intensely when she was on a film, but every extra inch showed on the screen, you had to stay ultra-slim.

'Is it in any of the others?' asked Ziggy, picking up the one she had thrown down a moment earlier. He began hunting through the papers, she knew when he found the picture, he stared at it while he read the story which always went with it, and he went on frowning.

'I'm sorry,' he said, looking up, and she shrugged.

'Wasn't your fault; just one of those things.'

'I shouldn't have lost my temper.'

At any other time it wouldn't have mattered so much, but Christie's film was one of the big successes of the festival; it had had a lot of publicity, she was very much in the news at the moment, the last thing she had wanted was this sort of exposure, and Ziggy knew it.

'I've got to go in to Antibes to have a drink with Carl,' he said, putting down the papers with a sigh. 'Carl will want to know about what happened; I'm surprised he hasn't been on the phone already.' Carl was in charge of the film publicity; he would have the unenviable task of denying the triangle story. 'I'll tell him the guy was drunk and got fresh with you, we don't even know his name. Carl will get to work playing it down, don't worry.' He poured himself some coffee. 'What are you going to do this morning?'

'Swim and relax for an hour and then get ready to go into Cannes for lunch.' She was wearing her bikini and the sun was beginning to be hot although it was only nine o'clock.

Erica and Johnny came out of the villa. They were both in jeans and T-shirts, and Erica was carrying a gaudy wicker basket. She looked at Christie quickly. 'How's the head? Better this morning?'

'Yes, thank you. Are you two going somewhere?'

'We thought we'd drive into the mountains today; we haven't had a chance to see anything but the coastal strip so far, we don't want to go home without taking a look at the view from those gorgeous mountains.'

Johnny looked at the basket of rolls and croissants and groaned. 'What I'd give for some waffles and syrup! Do you think that maid knows how to cook waffles?'

'I doubt it,' Christie said drily. 'She probably wouldn't even know what they were.' She got up, her slender body a delicate pale gold against the white of her bikini. 'I'm going to take a swim. See you all later.'

She found Kit and Janet in the pool; they raced each other from one end to the other and then played with a large red ball for half an hour, before Janet took Kit off to do some shopping with her in Antibes, leaving Christie sunbathing on one of the loungers by the pool. Her body was slack and tired in spite of a good night's sleep; she was worried about Ziggy, uncertain how to deal with the way he felt. Christie had always been insecure about herself, perhaps it had been that very uncertainty about her own identity that had made her want so badly to be an actress, and it was her inner personality that gave her the fragile beauty of which she herself was only half aware. When she looked into a mirror she saw the fine bones and wide, questioning eyes, the silvery hair and tender, curved mouth, and to her they added up to a lack of sexual impact. She would have preferred to be richer in colouring, full-breasted with long shapely legs. Christie was irritated by her own reflection, by her slightness and delicacy, the subtle tones of skin and hair, which she felt to be pallid and uninteresting. Her success in films sometimes amazed her, always puzzled her.

She lay with closed eyes on the lounger, her skin

glistening with sun-tan oil, her damp hair drying in
the morning sunshine, and felt herself slowing
down, relaxing, calming. The garden was full of
the scent of pine and cypress, the sky a vivid blue
and the air warm.

She heard a car drive through the gates, up the
winding drive towards the house. Kit and Janet
must be back, she thought, surprised. They had
only been gone ten minutes, surely? Opening her
eyes, she lazily lifted her arm to glance at her
watch, just as someone walked round the house on
to the paved terrace which led on to the pool area.
Christie turned her head, still relaxed in the
sunshine, and felt the sky go dark, her eyes cloud
with anger and pain. She sat up stiffly and
watched him walk towards her, so stunned that
she couldn't speak for a moment.

They had been divorced for four years and she
hadn't seen him for longer than that. Whenever he
visited Kit she made quite sure she was out of the
way, he had to let her know he was coming,
Christie had made it clear that she didn't want to
see him. Logan knew she hated him. He hadn't
challenged the divorce, he hadn't fought her for
custody of Kit, he had silently accepted both and
he had never tried to see her, they had only
communicated through their solicitors.

What was he doing here now?

CHAPTER TWO

HE halted a few feet from her lounger and stared at her, narrowed grey eyes flicking from her pale face to the almost naked curve of her body, and he hadn't changed. Her skin went cold as she absorbed the harsh, formidable strength which had always made him a man people backed away from when he frowned.

He held a newspaper clenched in one hand, she saw his white knuckles as he flung it at her.

'You've seen this, of course.'

The pages fluttered as they landed on her and she kicked the newspaper to the floor, an angry flush crawling into her cheeks. She wished she had brought a robe out with her, she was bitterly aware of those insulting grey eyes as they took in the tanned nudity her bikini made no pretence of covering. She was tempted to pick up the enormous flowered beach towel which was flung over the back of her lounger, but she wouldn't give Logan the satisfaction of knowing that he had unnerved her.

'I'm not responsible for the rubbish the newspapers print.'

He smiled contemptuously. 'And of course it wasn't your fault that these two guys fought over you? You were just an innocent bystander?'

She wasn't going to defend herself to him; make excuses, explain what had really happened. He wouldn't believe her and he would only sneer the way he was doing now; his hard mouth writhing with distaste which made her feel sick.

'What are *you* doing here?' she asked instead, mounting a counter-attack.

'I'm here to see my son,' he said shortly.

'Why didn't you ring first?' He usually did, he had never descended without warning before, why had he done so now? She hadn't even known he was in France. He had seen Kit in California a month ago. Logan lived in Los Angeles, but his business took him all over the world; he had a large and flourishing firm which he had built up himself, manufacturing photographic equipment of various kinds.

'I intended to—I had to come to Paris and meant to fly down here when I'd got through my business. Then I saw that story in the paper and caught the first plane to Nice.'

'You should still have rung first.' Christie stood up, trying to appear casual, and picked up the towel, hoping he wouldn't notice how her hand was trembling. He had always had a catastrophic effect on her, nothing had changed.

'I wanted to see for myself what sort of life-style you were inflicting on my son,' Logan said with biting scorn, watching as she wound the towel around her body, tucking the ends in firmly to anchor it beneath her arms, covering her breasts and falling to her feet like a toga.

Her flush deepened. 'My life-style is nothing to do with you!'

'That's where you're wrong! Anything that affects my son is of concern to me, I don't want Kit to grow up without any morals.'

'Get out of here!' Christie was almost speechless with insulted rage, she was shaking with a desire to hit him but afraid to lose control of herself that far. He was more than capable of hitting her back; Logan was violent, explosive, rows between them had always ended in a humiliating submission for her.

'Oh, not yet,' he said coolly, watching her flushed face with eyes that tore her apart. 'The garbage in that rag said you were living with one of the men—I forget his name, it was something ludicrous . . .'

'I'm not living with him, I'm staying in the same house!'

His black brows arched. He smiled and she seethed helplessly at that smile, at all it said. 'Call it what you like . . . I suppose it does sound better . . . but it means the newspaper had got it right, doesn't it? This guy . . .'

'Ziggy Molyneaux wrote the music for my latest film, that's why he's here—that's why we're both here, for the Cannes Film Festival. We aren't the only members of the team; the producer and director are here too.'

'Are you sleeping with them as well?'

Her face tightened. 'You've got a vile mind!'

'You must all have fun in the evenings—what do you do? Play Musical Bedrooms?' The mockery was iced, his smile savage. Logan was a tall man, broad-shouldered and lean-hipped, he had presence; people looked at him twice as he walked past them, but the harsh structure of his face and his thick black hair made him more impressive than charming.

'Ziggy is a friend of mine,' she began, and he laughed derisively. Christie's blue eyes burned with fury, she took a step towards him, her hands screwed up into fists, while Logan stood his ground, watching her, daring her to hit him.

'Don't bother with all these euphemisms for me,' he mocked. 'Your studio publicity department have done a good job on you, haven't they? I remember when you used to say what you meant, not wrap it up in glib nonsense. And don't get me wrong—I don't care how many "friends" you have. My only interest is in what all this is doing to Kit.'

'Kit is fine,' she burst out, shaking with rage.

'Oh, you think so?' Those brows arched again, dismissing her claim.

'I know so, he's my son . . .'

'Our son.' Logan cut across her stammered sentence in a voice so cold that she stopped talking and looked at him blankly. 'So far I haven't challenged your custody of him,' he went on in a hard voice. 'While he was just a baby he needed you; a small child needs its mother.' Logan's mother had died when he was very small. Christie had often wondered if that lack of female influence during his most impressionable years had hardened him. His father had been a remote, ambitious man more interested in success than anything else. He had not liked Christie, he hadn't welcomed her when she married his son, he was cold and hostile, not only to Christie but to all women. His wife's early death seemed to have cut him off from human contact; he kept even Logan at a distance, she had never seen any warmth between them, and Logan had been too much like his father.

Christie was worried by the implications of what Logan was saying; she stared at him searchingly, frowning.

'He's still a small boy and he still needs me,' she said fiercely, suddenly afraid.

'My son isn't growing up in this sort of circus. I hate to think what sort of ideas he's getting, watching you with all the men you have around you.' His eyes flicked over her again, insulting in their appraisal. 'You soon learnt how to be successful, didn't you? Three films in as many years! Not bad going for a comparative newcomer, and they've all been box office hits, I suppose. You've become quite a star—how many men helped you on your way, I wonder? Can you even remember?'

Christie had had enough. She walked past him, the edges of the towel fluttering. As she approached the villa she heard Janet's car turning into the drive; Kit waved to her from the back seat. The top was down and his dark hair ruffled by the breeze, it blew across his eyes and he brushed it away, staring past her. Janet parked on the forecourt outside the garage and Kit scrambled out, shouting, 'Daddy! Daddy!'

Christie didn't wait to see her son running to his father, to see Logan scoop him up into his arms and swing him round, laughing. She walked into the villa and Janet caught up with her, carrying several bags of shopping.

'I didn't know Mr Gray was arriving today,' she said curiously.

'Neither did I.' Christie tried to sound calm and composed, but it came out sharply and she felt Janet eyeing her sideways.

'Will he be staying for lunch?'

'Probably. I'm lunching in Cannes, remember. I'm going to get dressed now.' She halted in the marble-floored hall, frowning. 'Janet, stay with Kit and his father today, I'd rather Kit didn't leave the villa unless you're with them. If Mr Gray questions it, tell him I said you were to be with Kit all day.'

'Yes, of course,' said Janet, her voice even more curious.

Christie went up the stairs to her own room. From the garden she heard Kit talking excitedly, laughing, and just before she went into her room she heard Logan's deep voice murmuring; she couldn't hear what he said, but Kit laughed again, that helpless, gurgling laughter of childhood which means that a child is very happy. Christie bit her lip and closed the door. It was stupid to feel jealous; Logan was his father, she had never tried to stop Kit seeing him, she didn't want to deny her son anything, and she had a strong belief that a child needed to belong, to be part of a family; it gave Kit a sense of identity and security he might otherwise miss.

Christie had never seen them together before. She had always carefully avoided being there when Logan visited Kit. She went into the shower and turned on the spray, standing naked under it, letting the cool water run down her sun-flushed body, her eyes closed and behind her lids the image of Kit running, Logan picking him up, her son's happy laughter and obvious delight in seeing his father. She had not looked round, but she had heard them, she had felt the warmth between them, and it hurt her. She had always refused to ask Kit anything about his feelings for his father. Kit sometimes mentioned Logan, he told her what he and his father had done during their days together, but he was still quite inarticulate, he didn't put into words what Christie had just felt so strongly, the loving rapport between Kit and his father. It had surprised and shaken her; she had still thought of Logan as she remembered him from their marriage, she had not expected him to be so casual and relaxed with his son.

She dried herself, blowdried her long wet hair, and began to get dressed and put on her make-up. It took her quite a while; she would be on public display during the lunch. It was another aspect of the film's publicity for her to be seen lunching and dining around Cannes at the very best hotels. The dress she was wearing was very special; it had been created especially for her by a young American designer who had some original and stylish ideas, and the simplicity of the crisp white cotton was given flair by a high, pleated white ruff edged in gold which was echoed by a slim gold belt. It made Christie look young and innocent yet had a touch of rich sophistication; the ruff did not encircle her whole throat, it curved round and became the edging to a deep neckline which revealed half her breasts.

While she applied her make-up she thought back over her conversation with Logan, still bitterly angry about his accusations, and worried by his hint that he might challenge her custody of their son. It was the first time he had ever suggested taking charge of Kit, and it disturbed her. Would a court take Kit away from her? She couldn't believe it. She had been taking care of him since he was born; he was a healthy, happy little boy. When Christie was away from home she always took Kit with her, she spent as much time with him as she could, tried to give him a normal home life. She didn't allow Kit to get mixed up with her career; he wasn't involved in her publicity, she kept photographers and reporters well away from him. He kept regular hours; whatever Christie was doing, Janet saw to it that he was in bed and got up at the same times each day. It was so essential to a child to have a set routine, it made Kit feel more secure.

Logan couldn't step in now and snatch Kit away! The blue eyes looking back at her from the mirror were fierce with determination. She would speak to her lawyer as soon as she got home, check that Logan's threat was an empty one. She wasn't taking any chances with her son; she would fight tooth and nail to stop Logan taking him away from her.

When she went downstairs she found Ziggy in the spacious living-room, confronting Logan across the whole width of it with a wary expression. Kit wasn't in sight, to Christie's relief.

As Christie appeared, both men looked at her. Ziggy's eyes questioning, Logan's stare an icy examination under which she bristled while it swept from her gleaming, pale hair over the wickedly demure dress to her small feet in the fragile white sandals. Christie was just five foot two; her hands and feet were tiny, she had always felt dwarfed by Logan's height and strength. She refused to show it now; she put up her chin and glared back at him.

'I don't want Kit to leave the villa grounds—so if you want to spend the day with him, you'll have to spend it here.' She used a cool, clear voice and was pleased to find it sounding so self-confident. She didn't feel very confident; her insides were as weak as water.

'I planned to take him out to lunch somewhere special,' Logan retorted.

'I'm sorry,' she said without any real apology.

'I want to see him alone, I don't want that girl hanging around all the time, playing watchdog.'

'I do,' Christie told him. 'I trust Janet.' She didn't add what her tone implied, that she did not trust *him*; but his grey eyes narrowed and hardened as he listened. Looking away from him, Christie smiled at Ziggy.

'Ready? We'll be late if we don't leave now.'

Ziggy was only too happy to leave; he obviously found the loaded atmosphere alarming. He nodded and walked out of the open french windows into the garden. His hired car was parked on the drive, he walked towards it, and Logan watched him, mouth tight.

'So that's Ziggy Molyneaux.' He bit out the name with jeering distaste, and Christie was furious with him. 'I'd never have expected you to pick a guy like *that*,' he drawled, but she refused to pick him up on the comment. She wasn't going to give him a chance to run Ziggy down; the cold sarcasm in his face was quite enough. 'What's his real name?' asked Logan. 'Joe Smith? Fred Goldberg? Nobody in this world was ever called Ziggy Molyneaux at birth.'

'Next time you want to visit Kit, call first,' Christie said coldly, ignoring the insults, and turned to follow Ziggy to the car.

She didn't get very far. Logan's hand seized her arm, his long fingers biting into her flesh and making her wince as he held her back.

'Don't ever use that tone to me again!' he snarled, shaking her. She was caught off balance; her blue eyes wide in shock, her face almost as pale as the long, silky hair framing it. His voice, the harsh pressure of his hand, the nearness of that powerful body, took her breath away and carried her back to the years of their marriage, wiping out the time between as though it had never been.

She had been so young; too young to marry anyone—but particularly a man like Logan. He had been twelve years her senior. It didn't sound much, she had laughed off any warnings she was given about that age gap. At eighteen she had been so sure of everything, so confident. She wouldn't listen to advice, she was intoxicated with love, reeling into Logan's arms without any idea what she was doing, dying to go to bed with him and in too much of a hurry to know how it felt to wake up in his arms, to belong to him totally, be with him always, to have patience with anyone who tried to stop her. She had pushed aside what her parents said, what her friends said. What did they know about how she felt?

It had only taken a few months for her to realise what she had done. She had been too proud to admit her mistake to anyone; for a long time she had hidden it from her parents. They would have been sympathetic; she didn't doubt that, they loved her and would have been upset if they had known about the gap opening between her and Logan. Christie's pride wouldn't let her confide in them. It wasn't until she finally left Logan that they discovered what had been going on, and then they had been hurt because she hadn't told them.

Christie was no longer a girl of eighteen, though. She was a woman of twenty-seven. She pulled herself together, tugging her arm free from his grasp.

'Don't manhandle me—I had enough of that when we were married!' She took a deep breath, moving far enough away to be safe from him. 'I'll be out until around five, and I don't want to find you here when I get back!'

Logan didn't get a chance to answer, Christie turned on her heel and walked away, but although she hoped she looked calm she was still shaking. He still scared her; perhaps he would always scare her. He had a hard, sardonic personality even when he was not angry. When he was in a temper he could be terrifying. Christie couldn't remember seeing him laughing and casual, the way he had been with Kit earlier. In a way she was relieved to discover what a good relationship he had with their son; she didn't want Kit to grow up not knowing his father, she had already realised that much as she loved Kit and good though her own relationship with him was, he still needed a man in his life, a father figure to relate to, and learn from. It didn't matter so much while he was still so young; when he grew older she foresaw difficulties.

She got into the car beside Ziggy and the engine flared into life, they backed carefully down the drive. Logan stood on the terrace, watching them, his hands in his pockets and the breeze ruffling his black hair.

'You okay?' Ziggy asked her, and she started, looking round at him. His eyes were concerned, very blue in the sunlight, the sunny hair glistening.

'Do I look okay?' she asked wryly, and he grimaced.

'You look shattered, Christie.'

'And that's how I feel,' she said. 'Logan always did have that effect on me. One look at him and I'm so tense I can hear my teeth chattering.'

'I used to wonder why you'd divorced him,' Ziggy commented as he turned into the road and began to drive away. 'Now I wonder why you ever married him.'

'I was young and stupid,' Christie said bitterly, but there had been so much more to it than that. She had been young and wildly in love; she had burned for Logan with a fever she hadn't known how to cure. The depth of her passion was a gauge of the depth of her bitterness against him now.

'He's a hard man, isn't he?' Ziggy remarked, and she laughed without humour.

'Understatement! Yes, he's that, all right.'

'Attractive, I suppose,' Ziggy thought aloud. 'In a tough way; if you like the macho type, and I'd imagine most women do—especially younger women. He looks as if he likes his own way, though, I suppose he wasn't easy to live with.'

'He was hell to live with,' Christie said forcefully. 'He wanted to dictate everything I did; everything I wore, said, thought. I wasn't his wife, I was his possession, and he resented the fact that I wasn't happy to stay at home all day and wait for him to come back from whatever important business was keeping him away. He's the old-fashioned type. Women shouldn't want jobs, what do they want a career for? Logan wanted me to have children and be a docile housekeeper and hostess for him. He fought to stop me going on with my training at drama school. I'd only just started there when I met him and he tried to make me give it up. He simply couldn't understand why I wanted to be an actress.' It had been more than that, though. Logan had resented her wish to have an outside life; he had wanted her to narrow her world down to him and their home and the children he wanted her to have. Looking back, she sometimes wondered if he had deliberately chosen a very young girl because he thought she would be more pliable. For the first few months she had been so intensely in love with him that she had come very close to agreeing to give up her drama training, in fact. He had very nearly got what he wanted.

Ziggy listened to her long outburst, frowning. She had never been quite so frank with him before; she hadn't wanted to talk much about Logan. Ziggy had had some glimpses of how painful her marriage had been simply because when the subject came up she had never quite been able to hide her bitterness about her ex-husband, but she had refused to go into any details, partly because she wanted to forget the past and partly because of a confused sense of loyalty; not so much to Logan as to their marriage. What had happened had been private, between the two of them. Marriage is a

very private business and even the two involved
are not always aware of the whole picture; their
own view of it changes from time to time as they
change and mature. Events take on a meaning of
their own depending from where they are seen.
Christie had not wanted to betray herself or her
marriage to Ziggy, and she frowned as she realised
just how much she had just told him, regretting
her confidences.

'What's wrong, Christie?' Ziggy asked abruptly,
slowing down in the crowded traffic going into
Cannes. 'You're upset about something, aren't
you? What did he say to you?'

She swallowed. 'He hinted that he was going to
ask for custody of Kit . . .'

'He can't do that,' Ziggy broke out, looking
round at her. 'You've had Kit since he was born;
he's never lived with his father, has he?'

She shook her head. 'No, I left Logan before
Kit was born. Logan saw that picture in the paper;
he says he's going to claim I'm not a fit person to
have Kit, my life-style is too immoral.' She tried to
make it sound ridiculous, to laugh, but her mouth
was trembling.

Ziggy put a hand over hers, squeezing her
fingers gently. 'Don't look so scared. We won't let
him take Kit away from you. Christie, marry me
and we'll make Kit a happy home, I'll take care of
both of you and we'll fight Logan Gray together.'

Christie stared at the glitter of the blue sea on
their right, watching the dance of white sails across
it as yachts skimmed along the shore. She was
tempted to say yes. She felt so shaken by seeing
Logan again. She needed some sort of reassuring

presence in her life, a man to make a safety curtain between herself and Logan, and she trusted Ziggy. More than that, she loved him, he had become very much a part of her life, and they had so much in common, their lives would merge beautifully, they already had the same friends, the film world in common, a shared love of music and the theatre. Christie caught herself up, her face uneasy. She was trying to talk herself into accepting his proposal. Logan had made her running scared. She was bolting for safety into Ziggy's arms.

Wryly she said: 'Don't tempt me, Ziggy—I might say yes on impulse and it wouldn't be fair to you, you'd reproach me later.'

'Of course I wouldn't,' he said quickly. 'How could I? You've been totally frank with me, you haven't pretended ... marry me, Christie, on your own terms. I'm absolutely certain we'll be happy together. I couldn't be more sure.' He was smiling sideways at her, his eyes vivid, as blue as the sea with the sun on it, his blond hair gilded by that southern light.

Slowly she nodded, and Ziggy's eyes blazed. Christie at once felt a qualm of doubt, of uneasiness—had she made another disastrous mistake? She opened her lips to withdraw the silent agreement, to qualify it, and Ziggy put a hand over her mouth.

'No, don't say anything, don't spoil it.' He looked away at the shimmering blue horizon, smiling. 'What a miraculous day it is—look at that light! On days like this I feel as if I could fly. You know, I write totally different music when the sun is shining—when it's rainy or windy my head seems to follow suit and turn out stuff that has storm in it. I think I must have been influenced by the mood music they used to play in films . . .'

He talked on as he drove them to the hotel at which they were having lunch with various important names in the film world, and Christie sat listening to the torrent of excited, exultant words, her face troubled.

A small crowd had gathered to watch the arrivals of other film celebrities for the lunch. The police were out in force, holding the pushing bodies back, but Ziggy and Christie still had to fight their way through a battery of pressmen with flashlights going off in their faces and questions jabbered at them from all corners. They dashed into the hotel, smiling tightly, ignoring the questions, but during the lunch they came in for a lot of teasing on the same subject, with a somewhat different approach. Several of the actresses present were amused by the fact that Carol Heaven's latest had chased Christie.

'Darling, did she throw a wingding? I wish I'd seen her face; isn't she gruesome when she's in a temper?' The actress sipped her wine, eyeing Christie teasingly.

'She's gruesome when she isn't,' someone else said, and they all laughed.

'Watch out for her,' Christie was warned. 'She'll carve you up if she can. She's a grudge-bearer.'

'She's slipping down the ladder,' a producer said wryly. 'And she knows it and there's nothing she can do about it. She could never sing, she can't act, and that famous body is middle-aged now. She's had it.'

Christie shivered. 'Don't!' She didn't like Carol, but she felt intensely sorry for her. There were many aspects of the film world that she didn't like; the callous dismissal of yesterday's stars was one of them, everything was instant, now, and the film hierarchy had no memory. They loved you passionately until your box office appeal slipped, and then they couldn't even remember your name, they were always in a meeting when you rang, you became a professional leper.

'Bud's a smart kid,' another of the producers murmured to her through a display of too perfect spring flowers which occupied the centre of the table. Crystal glasses, silver, and damask napkins— the whole table looked like a film set, and every guest was too elegant, too carefully on his or her best behaviour; even the malice was delivered with a sweet smile. 'I hear he's been talking his head off to the press ever since they picked up the story.'

'What story?' Christie exploded, and they all looked at her expectantly, eyes avidly interested in her flushed face and stormy expression. 'He was drunk, he tried to paw me and Ziggy slugged him. That's it, the whole story, period. 'I'd never seen him before, I don't know him from Adam. It's all a flammed-up story.'

'That's not how he tells it.'

'Then he's a goddamned liar,' said Ziggy, lazily, without emotion.

'Bud's ambitious, he's hoping to get a start in films, you can't blame the kid for trying. Give him A for effort, Ziggy—this is a chance in a million for him. Nice publicity for an unknown kid; he's got something going for him, he'd be a fool to let it go.' The bald-headed man smiled blandly; he was famous for smiling most when he was at his most deadly. Christie watched him with intuitive suspicion and wondered if he was considering giving Carol Heaven's young man a part in one of his current productions. He caught her eye and gave her a warm, loving smile. His bald head was probably the only honest part of him; even his teeth were false, and his smile was the phoniest thing about him.

As she and Ziggy drove back to the villa she stared at the crowded road ahead of them and said: 'When we leave here I'm going to London and I'm going to sit there and wait until that agent of mine comes up with a part in a play. I'm not making any more films. I've had those people; they make me ill.'

'They're just people,' Ziggy said tolerantly, and she looked at him with impatience.

'Do me a favour, Ziggy—don't feed me saccharine. If they are people, give me sharks any time. At least *they* don't pretend to be interested in anything but eating you!'

CHAPTER THREE

'WHEN shall we announce our engagement?' asked Ziggy, turning his car into the coastal road which ran along the promontory of Cap d'Antibes. The rocky finger of land projected into the blue water with Cannes on one side and the Bay of the Angels, dominated by Nice, on the other, and across the sunlit sea tacked white-sailed yachts and bronzed young men on sailboards.

'Not while we're here,' Christie said, frowning. Cap d'Antibes was the exclusive preserve of the rich who preferred to get away from the bars and nightclubs, the wandering crowds of holiday-makers, the cars and carnival atmosphere of the rest of the Côte d'Azur. Christie felt unreal here; she didn't want to find the world's press camping on their doorstep. It would be wiser to let the press forget the incident at the Casino before they announced their engagement.

'In London?'

'Do we have to announce it at all? I don't want it turning into a three-ring circus. I've had quite enough of the press.' She looked across the sea; the view was spectacular from here but she was longing to get back to London. She hadn't been home for what seemed an eternity. Before she left California she had given up the lease of her apartment at Malibu and she intended to buy a house in London. Kit would be starting school this autumn; she wanted to give him a settled home and friends, a normal life. Kit had loved it at Malibu, of course, just as he loved it here; at times Christie was strongly reminded of California when she watched the crowded beaches. The only difference was that here the beach was narrow and pebbled, whereas the Californian coast boasted wide, curving sandy beaches, but they had much else in common. They were both laid-back, uninhibited, untrammelled by convention—people wore as little as possible and spent as much time as they could in the sunlight; swimming and sailboarding and sailing. There was a relaxed, holiday air; most of the girls on the beaches went topless and had deep, gleaming tans. The cult of youth was paramount; the sun-worshippers flocked to the sea half-naked, blinded by the dazzle of sunlight on blue water and white buildings, there was no sense of time, no need to do anything but enjoy yourself. But it was all an illusion. You stepped out of ordinary life when you came to a place like this; but sooner or later you had to step back into it, and Christie couldn't wait to do so. She had never imagined she would tire of the sun, but she knew she had.

Ziggy turned into the drive of the villa. Cap d'Antibes was full of such villas; palatial, hidden away behind walls and hedges, to give their owners a sense of privacy. As the car purred up the drive Christie watched the drooping green branches of a willow brush across the windscreen and through their delicate leaves saw the white walls of the house, and Kit and Janet sitting at the table on the patio, playing dominoes.

Her heart turned over in relief. Logan wasn't with them, he had gone. She sighed, and Ziggy gave her a sharp, intent look.

'What's wrong?'

'Nothing, I'm just tired.' She was more weary than tired; over the last three years her life had bounced from one surprise to another. She had been permanently at work on films, she hadn't had a chance to step aside and look at the way her life was going, and she needed that long-distance self-inspection.

Sometimes she felt a hundred, she had a shock of disbelief every time she reminded herself that she was only twenty-seven; time seemed to have whizzed past at a tremendous rate without her noticing the years passing. It seemed only yesterday that she had been eighteen and in her first year at drama school; wide-eyed and walking on air because of the excitement of it all. She had met Logan during her first term; it had been a bleak winter, but she had been lit up inside with the euphoria of being in London learning how to act; she had been ready to fall in love with anyone, perhaps. Such heady excitement makes anything seem possible; she had felt that the world was her oyster, she had no time for doubts or questions, she was young and she was too dumb to know how young she was.

'You can't get married,' her father had said blankly. 'What about the drama school? Are you giving that up?' and of course she had laughed and said: 'No, of course not,' because it hadn't entered her head that Logan would want her to give up the dream she had had for years and which was just within her grasp. She hadn't believed in failure, in those far-off days. She had known with absolute certainty that she was going to find success in her career.

She wished she had some of that confidence now. Only total innocence could give you that, though, and she knew too much about the pitfalls and rocks of her profession now. Her success in films had not been what she had been looking for; she hadn't been doing what she wanted to do, she hadn't found the satisfaction she had dreamed about. She had earned a lot of money, met a lot of famous people, been to fabulous places—at first that had seemed wildly exciting, too, but gradually she had realised that she was cheating herself, deceiving herself. She had wandered off into a glittering bazaar and lost the way; she had to get back on the right road again, and this time she knew it was going to be much harder. The scales had fallen from her eyes, she saw much more clearly; she knew what she had not known at eighteen, that nothing worthwhile is that easy. She wished she had known that when Logan asked her to marry him.

It had seemed easy enough, then, to transfer her drama course from London to Los Angeles, so that she could combine marriage with a career training. Looking back, she suspected that Logan had regarded her drama course in the nature of a hobby which would give her something to do while he was at work and help her to settle into a new life in a new country. By the time they had been married for a year he had begun trying to persuade her to give up the course, have a baby and concentrate on their private life. She had begun to discover that Logan was a possessive man; he resented the friends she had made at drama school, he objected to the hours she had to put in during the evenings and at weekends. You couldn't just work nine to four; you had to rehearse for school productions in your spare time and you had to visit some of the excellent professional productions put on in the city. It was all part of your training, and she explained that to Logan without making any impact. He became more and more impatient, more and more angry.

'Marriage is a full-time commitment,' he had insisted, and Christie had tried to laugh that off.

'That's old-fashioned . . .' Laughing hadn't helped, of course; trying to tease him out of his attitudes simply made him angrier. They hadn't been able to talk calmly; they hadn't known each other long enough and their reactions were too bedevilled by emotions which Christie, at least, didn't understand and couldn't control. They always ended up shouting at each other from opposite sides of a vast gulf. She did not see his point of view; Logan couldn't see hers. The years between them had made too wide a gulf. Christie was ambitious and eager to learn about life before she narrowed her horizons to a family. Logan was set on having children, a peaceful home where he could get away from the pressures of his own work and forget the outside world.

They had married for very different reasons, with very different expectations—their perspectives of life were from distant angles. Christie had met him at precisely the moment when she was just entering that adult world of glitter and anticipation, of dream and boundless possibility, when anything might happen—and Logan had been a part of that, not something separate. She had got married with no real idea of what she was doing. Of course, she would have denied it then—she had denied it to Logan, to her parents, even to herself. She had believed that she was madly in love and she knew what she was doing.

Well, the emotion itself had been real enough— she had been crazy about Logan. He had been so glamorous, not a gauche boy like all the other boy-friends she had ever had, but a strong adult man, with a personality that dazzled her; sophisticated, experienced, at times tender, at other times white-hot with passion. She had been flattered by his pursuit, intrigued by the glimpses she got of what lay beneath his surface, by her first realisation of the separateness, the apartness, which makes a lover a puzzle one longs to solve. When she married Logan she had been walking blindfold into a dark maze; but she had not known it.

Logan's resentment of her other world had grown gradually; he began to demand that she give up her drama course, instead of merely suggesting it. He was jealous of the young men she acted with, had sandwiches with at lunchtime, went to rehearsal with when school was over. She came home late sometimes; when you had been rehearsing for hours and everyone else went on to have a drink and talk excitedly about the play you were doing, it was hard to leave and go on home.

Slowly she realised that it wasn't working. She

was trying to keep a foot in two worlds. If she had been older or Logan more understanding, it might have been okay, they could have talked it out, but Logan tried to override her; he tried to use force instead of persuasion. When they had a row it was hard for Christie to hold her own against him; she couldn't match his biting sarcasm, his dominating force. He made her feel very young and inadequate. For the first time she really became aware of the difference in their ages.

'Don't treat me like a child!' she shouted at him once, and he looked at her with what she felt was contempt.

'Don't behave like one!'

Her friends at drama school treated her as an equal, of course; coming home from being one among many equals Christie resented being treated as a child by her husband, especially when she began to realise that Logan had never taken her career seriously; he had been giving her time to come around to his point of view, that was all.

Their quarrels became more violent, more unreasonable, when she was offered a professional role after she left the drama school, and she found Logan prepared to fight tooth and nail to stop her accepting it.

'No,' he said. 'You've had three years of drama—when are you going to have a baby? What do you think marriage means? We share a roof and a bed, but so far that's been all. I want children while I'm young enough to enjoy them.'

Christie had tried to keep her temper. 'Logan, I must have a chance to see if I can succeed on the stage—let me take this job.'

'If you take this one, there'll be another along, and then another—how many years do you expect me to wait?'

'Is that all I mean to you? Someone to have your baby?' Her resentment showed in her sharp, bitter voice.

'I see little enough of you now,' Logan flung back at her. 'If you're working in a theatre every night of the week, I'll see even less.'

'You have a job, you often go away for a week at a time, you don't expect me to complain, but that's different, isn't it? Because you're a man . . .' she was shouting, too confused to be coherent; she met anger with anger, as blindly as she had met love with love. 'You keep telling me what you want,' she had shouted. 'What about what I want? I'm only twenty-one, there's plenty of time to have a baby, but parts like this one don't grow on every tree, I may never get such a terrific chance again if I turn this down.'

'When we got married you wanted to have children,' Logan had reminded her grimly, and it had been true, but when they talked about it then it had seemed a distant daydream, something for the future; she hadn't meant that she wanted to have a baby right away and neither had he seemed to expect it. It had been a lovely idea to murmur as they danced cheek to cheek or walked slowly in some London park that winter: 'If we have a son what shall we call him? I wonder if he'll be dark, like you, I hope so . . .' The drive of her energy had not gone into her marriage, though; it had gone into building her career, but she had talked to Logan about that, too.

She could remember quiet days when they were alone, during their early marriage, at a weekend or during the summer vacations, when they had relaxed together, Christie reading a play or a book of poetry or the life of some famous actress, while Logan read a book of his own, and looked up now and then to smile at her and listen when she read him something, laughing. 'I'd love to play that part,' she would say, and he would nod. Or she would say: '*I* feel like that when I'm on a stage . . .' and Logan would listen sympathetically as she talked about it, but she realised, looking back, that he had been indulging her, amused by her dreams, convinced she would grow out of them. He had never taken her career seriously.

'One day I may want children, but not yet,' she had said then, unable to add what she was thinking: how could she have a child before she felt fully adult herself? It would have sounded so silly; she was old enough to get married, after all, and perhaps that wasn't what she had meant at all, perhaps she simply felt that she didn't yet know enough about herself as an adult to feel capable of handling a child. Acting was a form of self-discovery; it was a voyage into oneself which uncovered things the conscious mind did not necessarily know. Christie had learnt enough about herself by then to know how little she knew about life and about other people, including Logan, but she couldn't put all that into words, she could only stare bitterly at him, choked with all the emotional turmoil she was unable to explain.

'You married me, I have some say in what you do,' Logan bit out, very flushed.

'You don't own me!'

'Then maybe it's time I did,' he said, and as she tried to push him away his temper flared again and he knocked her backwards on to their bed, the full weight of his body pinning her down as she tried to struggle up.

'Let go of me, Logan, I don't want . . .'

'I'm sick of hearing what you want and don't want! I'm sick of a wife who spends more time with other men than me . . .'

'We were rehearsing!'

He snarled his derision, his grey eyes contemptuous. 'In a bar?'

'I've told you, we always go for a drink afterwards—all of us, the whole cast! I can't get out of going and anyway, why should I? Why should I stay out of all the social life at the college? Why . . .'

'Because you're married,' Logan said tersely, and she was silent, facing the root of the problem. Her career and her marriage did not merge; there was no way she could meet the demands of both.

'You're not going to take this part,' Logan said curtly. 'You're going to give up any idea of a career and have a baby, afterwards we can see how you feel, when the baby's old enough . . .'

'No, Logan—I won't have a baby! I don't want one, and it would be wrong to have a child without wanting it. I'd resent it.'

'I'll resent it if you don't,' said Logan, and that made his position clear; they stared at each other across an abyss, like separated enemies.

'That's up to you,' Christie had said huskily, and tried to get up, pushing at his shoulders. 'We should never have got married in the first place . . .'

Logan had gone pale, his face stiffening into a cold mask. Logan's rage was as white-hot and dangerous as his desire, and she had inflamed both with her cool retort, but she didn't realise until later that she had provoked his violence. When he grabbed her nightdress, ripping it as she tried to struggle free, she almost screamed: 'I'll hate you!' but he was too angry to listen any more, her writhing body was held down while she fought and yelled, and he took her forcibly without tenderness. Their marriage was over within a few minutes. Christie could hardly bear to look at him again, she left him next day and started divorce proceedings shortly afterwards.

She didn't know for several months that she was pregnant; that had been unexpected. She had been on the pill and it was a considerable shock to her to realise that she had conceived, on that particular night, although her doctor later suggested that she might have forgotten to take the pill during the last eventful days of her school career. It was possible. She had been so disturbed that she had even suspected Logan of substituting some other pills for the ones she had been prescribed, but angry as she was with him she didn't think he was capable of something like that. Logan wasn't devious or sneaky; it was out of character.

By the time she had realised that she was going to have a baby, she was already in rehearsal for the part she had been offered, but luckily it would be a short run, a mere six weeks, and her

pregnancy wouldn't show for some months. That
was a relief because she needed the money; she
wouldn't take any from Logan, she needed to be
financially independent. The play was a mild
success and brought her a film offer which she
accepted since filming wouldn't begin until after
she had had the baby. Logan found out she was
pregnant, eventually, and tried to see her—but
Christie refused. She felt too bitter about that last
night together and about the result of it. She did
not want to have his child, and during the months
while she waited for the birth she brooded for
hours about Logan's selfishness and egotism.

Then she had Kit, and her whole perspective
shifted again; she rediscovered love in a new form
with a new tenderness and sense of belonging, but
although Logan visited her in the hospital she still
refused to see him. She could not forgive him. The
divorce went through, she allowed Logan to see
his son whenever he chose as long as he warned
her in advance, and within a few months she was
working on her first film. She had taken that part
because she needed the money and it was the only
offer she had had made to her. She had intended
to go back into the theatre afterwards, but a
second part in a film had come along and she had
been persuaded to take that. Logan made her a
very handsome allowance for herself and Kit; but
she put it all into a trust fund for Kit, she wouldn't
touch it. She wanted nothing from Logan. She
could keep herself and her son by her own efforts,
and she meant to do so.

She felt now that if she did not break out of
films and try to succeed in the theatre she might

never do so, and she still felt that driving impulse to act on a stage. She had not forgotten her old dream—she had merely mislaid it, which was another reason for her resentment with Logan. She wouldn't have taken that first film part if she hadn't needed the money for Kit. Logan had driven her into films.

While she was absorbed in her memories Ziggy had parked the car outside the garage, Christie had got out and walked over to the patio, still thinking, and it wasn't until Kit jumped up and hugged her that she came fully back to the present, smiling at him before giving him a kiss.

'Miss me?'

'Huh,' he said, rubbing his head on her waist in inarticulate agreement. 'Come and play with Janet and me.'

Christie sat down at the table. 'Cheating as usual?' she asked Janet, who laughed.

Kit said indignantly: 'I wasn't cheating; I forgot I had a two—I did, I just forgot.'

'He forgot,' Janet said drily, and Christie grinned at her.

'I haven't got anything on for the rest of the day, if you'd like to take a few hours off.' She always tried to give Janet plenty of free time, Kit must be tiring.

Janet got to her feet, her face lighting up. 'If you're sure, I would like to drive up to the mountains and take a look at Gourdon while we're here. I've heard that the chateau is fabulous and the view from up there takes your breath away.'

'Off you go, then, have a good time. If you want

to have dinner out, that's fine. We'll expect you when we see you.' Christie enjoyed putting her son to bed; she often felt guilty about the amount of time she spent away from him.

For the next hour she played with Kit and then they swam for a while until it was time Kit had his tea and went to bed. Erica and her husband had been out all day; they arrived while Christie was sitting on Kit's bed telling him a bedtime story. His skin was flushed rosily from his bath, his eyelids heavy, but he struggled to stay awake to hear the end of her story. Christie brushed the dark hair back from his forehead, getting up.

'Goodnight, sleep tight,' she said softly, and Kit drowsily repeated the phrase; it was part of his routine, children are creatures of habit, they don't like their secure pattern to be broken.

Christie was frowning as she went downstairs. How would Kit feel about the move to London? He had always lived in California, near the sun and sea; he was going to find a very different sort of world, a very new life, back in London. He knew his grandparents, of course; they had been over to visit Christie several times during the past couple of years, and they were one of the reasons Christie had for moving back to England. She wanted to be near them, Kit needed to have a wider family circle than he had at present. At the moment, they led a strange sort of life; she didn't see enough of Kit and it preyed on her mind. If she was on the stage she would be able to spend most of the day with him when she wasn't rehearsing. She would only be working at night except when they played a matinee.

She had earned enough money from her three films to be able to live very comfortably for a long time without working at all, and she would see far more of Kit from now on, as well as visiting her parents more often.

There was one aspect of the move that troubled her, but she didn't dwell on it. Kit would see far less of his father; Logan lived in Los Angeles, he wouldn't be able to visit Kit so often once they were in London, and in one sense that was a relief because Christie was worried by Logan's threat to take custody away from her, but at the same time she felt guilty about depriving Kit of his father's frequent visits, and she was nervous about Logan's reaction once he discovered that she had taken his son to England. Logan was capable of a savage fury that in the past she had only been able to meet with an answering rage; she wouldn't like to be around when he realised she and Kit had left California and were hundreds of miles away. She was five years older than she had been when their marriage ended; but she still found Logan scary.

She found Erica in the immaculate modern kitchen, surveying the cold food which the maid had left for their dinner. 'Feel like dinner out tonight?' asked Erica wryly.

'I can't go out—Janet is taking the evening off. But you and Johnny can go if you can't face another cold meal—or I could make omelettes, or maybe spaghetti?' Christie enjoyed cooking but had little time for it.

'I'm trying to sample as much French cooking as I can while we're here,' Erica said slowly. 'Some of the restaurants around here are out of this world. It's playing havoc with my diet, but I can't resist. You know me . . . no will power.' Erica was lazy and tolerant, like Ziggy; she took life as it came and enjoyed herself. Christie sometimes envied her that ability to drift with the tide; it wasn't an attitude Christie could imitate, she wasn't capable of taking life that lightly. No doubt if she had been, she would have fallen in with Logan's wishes and had his child and stayed at home without hankering for the theatre, and her whole life would have been so different.

'Weren't you ever ambitious, Erica?' she asked curiously, beginning to prepare the dressing for the salad she meant to eat.

Erica took a stick of celery and crunched thoughtfully. 'When I was a kid I sometimes dreamt of being a famous opera singer; but I soon realised I didn't have the voice for it. I do okay; I make a living and I have fun. You can only do what you're capable of doing, can't you?' There was slight defensiveness in her voice as though she thought Christie was criticising her. 'I'm not like you,' she added. 'You've got to have the drive to get to the top and I just don't have it. I don't even want it; all it gives you is ulcers and I can do without them. I guess you have to know yourself, that's the secret. That's why I don't have kids—I'd be a rotten mother, why inflict myself on some poor child?'

Christie poured the lightly beaten dressing over the salad, frowning. 'It isn't easy to know yourself, though, is it? We never see ourselves the way other people see us; they're looking from the outside, we're on the inside looking out.'

Erica studied her profile. 'What's bothering you? That ex-husband of yours? He was here most of the day with Kit, wasn't he? Ziggy mentioned it just now. Did it bug you, seeing him again?'

Christie grimaced. 'I guess so.'

'Ziggy didn't take to him, but then he wouldn't, would he?' Erica laughed, and Christie forced a smile. 'Can I ask a personal question?' Erica didn't wait for Christie to answer, she went ahead and asked: 'Do you plan to marry Ziggy?'

Christie picked up the salad bowl, her head averted. 'We'll tell you when we've decided,' she said lightly, but her tone closed the door on further discussion and she walked away to start laying the dining-room table, leaving Erica behind.

Ziggy had much in common with his sister on the surface; but his music revealed a very different personality, and it was that Ziggy that Christie loved, the gentle, sensitive, almost melancholy man who could make you cry with his music. If Erica had anything in common with that Ziggy, Christie had yet to see it, and Ziggy himself rarely showed his secret inner self in company. When he was with strangers he was as lazily entertaining and charming as Erica could be; he publicly avoided any depth or emotion, perhaps he was afraid of showing his real self. With some people it is unwise to admit vulnerability; they take advantage of it, they see it as weakness.

It was Ziggy's vulnerability that made Christie feel so guilty about him. He wasn't the only man in the past four years who had pursued her or claimed to be in love with her, but she had never cared for the others the way she did for Ziggy. She loved him enough to wish she loved him more or that he felt less deeply about her. She did not want to hurt him, yet couldn't see any way of avoiding it except by hurting him badly for a short time by finishing their relationship, in the hope that he might get over her. Ziggy had played it so lightly until now; she hadn't realised how serious he was, he had hidden the depth of his feelings from her, as he hid his true depth from strangers. Ziggy was a secretive man, a deceptive man. Christie felt now that she had never really known him. Or was she just a very poor judge of people? What had she ever really understood about Logan? What did she understand about him now? Actors aren't the only ones who wear masks. All human beings need them at some time in their lives; many people spend their whole lives behind masks.

During their marriage she had been too young to penetrate Logan's mask. It had been his mask she fell in love with, she realised with a sudden shock. It hadn't been the man at all—she didn't have any idea what he was like behind the glamour and hard sophistication.

How strange, she thought wryly, to suddenly start wondering about a man you had been married to for three years! Why hadn't she asked questions before? Why hadn't she thought more deeply about his motives, his reasons for behaving as he did?

But that was easy to answer—she had been too young, she had been too busy trying to work herself out, she hadn't had energy or time to work out anyone else, she had been self-obsessed, blinded by dreams. Her mouth compressed, remembering her younger self; she had been a self-centred idiot, Logan must have been crazy to marry her. Hadn't he realised how young she was, how unfit for marriage?

They all had supper together. Erica dominated the conversation; lovingly describing great meals she had had since they arrived in the South of France, and rueful over the salad and cold meat they were eating now. Ziggy winked at Christie as he refilled her glass.

'You can't complain about the wine,' he told his sister, and Erica held out her glass, grinning.

'I wasn't. The wine is great. I can't get over the price of wine here—I wish we could take crates and crates of it back home, don't you, Johnny?'

Johnny agreed; he agreed with everything his wife said, he liked a peaceful life, and he found Erica amusing; she always made him laugh, and he didn't seem to regret their childless state either. Christie sometimes wondered if Erica was the child in that family; Johnny frequently acted like an indulgent parent rather than a husband. It certainly seemed to make them both happy; people choose strange ways of life, the only thing that matters is that their living pattern satisfies them. Christie wasn't going to act the 'censor; her own way of life had too many flaws for her to do that.

Ziggy was very happy tonight, whenever he looked at Christie his blue eyes glowed with happiness. Christie went to bed early because feeling Ziggy's eyes on her made her guilty and uneasy. Could they be happy? She had married for the wrong reasons once; she was very much afraid of doing the same thing again. At least this time she knew what she was doing; she wasn't fooling herself or Ziggy. She had been honest with him, he knew the risk he was taking. Did that excuse her for letting him take that risk, though? If Ziggy was in love with her he might be blind to the possible consequences, the way she had been when she married Logan. A man who is in love can convince himself against all reason. She had told Ziggy she wasn't in love with him—but did Ziggy still hope she might fall in love once they were married? Did Ziggy secretly hope for more than she could give him? And when she failed to return his love the way he wanted her to, would he blame her, in spite of her honesty now?

She undressed and lay in bed, her mind too active for sleep. Why had Logan married her? The question kept returning, haunting her. She turned over, irritated with herself. She had to get some sleep, she would be dead in the morning if she didn't sleep now. She didn't want to think about Logan. He was the past. She should be thinking about the future. What did it matter now why he had married her?

She wished she hadn't been at the villa when he appeared that morning. If she and Ziggy had left earlier they wouldn't have seen him, and he wouldn't be on her mind. She had enough to worry about without adding Logan Gray to her other problems.

CHAPTER FOUR

'But if we live in London, I won't see Daddy,' said Kit, his lip trembling, and Christie quickly put her arms round him, her cheek on his hair.

'Of course you will! He'll visit you, he often goes to London on business, you know that. Didn't he bring you a red London bus last time he went? And the time before that, a London taxi for your car collection?' Kit was on her lap and she rocked him slightly, hugging him. 'You'll probably see him just as often as you ever did.'

Kit looked up at her, unconvinced, accusing, and she felt terrible as she met his eyes; the eyes he had inherited from his father, although they were more blue than grey as yet, each year their colour seemed to fade a little. When he was born he had had eyes of dark blue, almost navy blue; now they were very light.

'Why do we have to go? I don't want to, I don't want to live in London, why do we have to go?'

'Because of my work,' Christie said uneasily. 'I told you, Kit—I have to live in London if I'm going to act on the stage instead of in films, and that's what I want to do now.'

'Is Janet coming?'

'Of course she is!' Christie had already talked to Janet, who had been perfectly happy to live in London. 'But you'll be going to school in the autumn, that will be fun, won't it? You'll have lots of friends and you'll be very busy.'

'There isn't any beach in London,' Kit complained, and she had to admit that there wasn't, but they would visit the sea as often as they could. It wasn't far from London; just a few hours away. That didn't make Kit any happier; he had grown up with a beach on his doorstep, he had his breakfast every morning watching the waves cream over the sand and was out there, swimming like a fish already, for a good part of the day in summer.

'But there's lots to do in London,' she protested, and tried to remember all the exciting places and things he would discover, but Kit wasn't impressed. He went back to his immediate response. 'Daddy will be in Los Angeles, I won't see him.'

Janet came out of the villa in time to hear that. She made a wry face at Christie over Kit's head, then said to him brightly: 'Coming for a drive? I've got some shopping to do in Antibes. When I've done that we could go find a beach and swim. It would make a change from the pool, wouldn't it?'

Kit clambered off his mother's lap, nodding. 'Okay.'

'Run and get your swimming trunks, then,' Janet told him, and when he had darted back into the villa she looked at Christie sympathetically. 'He'll get used to the idea; kids are so conservative, they hate changes.'

'Especially boys,' said Christie with a sigh. 'And they turn into men, which explains a lot.'

Janet laughed. 'How true!' She hesitated, then asked: 'Does Mr Gray know you plan to move to London?'

'No,' said Christie. 'And I'm not in a hurry to

have him find out. It's just as well he saw Kit yesterday before I told Kit we were moving to London, I don't suppose we'll see Mr Gray again for a while, and by then we'll have moved.'

Janet didn't say anything, but her face was eloquent and Christie viewed her defiantly. She knew what Janet was thinking—when Logan found out, there would be trouble. Christie wanted to put off any confrontation with him about this move to London; Logan was a daunting adversary. At the moment she didn't feel up to any more arguments. This morning she had woken up feeling tired and oddly depressed. Her jaw ached with the constant smiling and talking she had been doing since they got here. She had been on public display for too many hours. She needed some peace and quiet; she needed to be alone.

Ziggy was at the premiere of a film starring a friend of his; he had worked on the music score and had been officially invited. He had wanted Christie to go with him, but she had pleaded her way out of that, using her headache as an excuse. Erica had offered to stay with her for the morning, but Christie had insisted that Erica and Johnny go ahead with their plan of driving through the mountains in search of some fabled restaurant whose menu was world-famous.

The villa was quiet and tranquil in the May sunshine. Christie meant to relax and do absolutely nothing for a few hours.

Kit and Janet left, laden down with swimming gear, beach ball, bucket and spade, enormous beach towels and some cans of Coke. Kit had cheered up enough to wave and smile as they drove out of the gate. At his age moods came and went like spring sunshine. Christie was sure that once he was at school in London, visiting his grandparents and collecting some friends of his own age, he would settle down happily enough, but she still felt guilty about him. Kit was the person who mattered most in the world to her; he was the private centre of her life, she badly wanted him to be happy and she hated to feel that she was depriving him of anything. He was a lively, active child and he always seemed to be happy; what had her split with his father done to him, though? Kit was reserved on that particular subject; he either couldn't or wouldn't put into words how he felt, and Christie was afraid of asking questions to which the answers might be painful.

Sighing, Christie moved one of the padded loungers fully into the sun, and lay down; her slender, bikini-clad body relaxing. There was a gentle warmth in the air today, the Riviera heat hadn't yet begun, although in a month the sun would have a fierce, brazen insistence. A breeze stroked the cypress hedges which rippled like the fur of a silky cat, there was a scent of pine and warm grass, early swallows looped across the blue sky. Christie hadn't slept too well last night, she had had too much on her mind. She closed her eyes and let the tranquillity of the garden sink into her.

She must have slept, although she wasn't aware of it, because when she became aware again her mind was full of the remnants of dreams—voices, faces, an emotion which still echoed inside her, although as she opened her eyes they all faded and she stared at the man standing in front of her as though he was a part of those dreams which had broken through into the real world and become flesh and blood. For a minute she was held in suspension; her blue eyes wide and shocked, her silvery hair fanned around her face by the breeze.

Logan watched her startled face, then his eyes coolly drifted down over the golden curve of her tanned body in the brief black bikini, and her immobility broke up under the stab of sharp sensual awareness; her pulses beat in the blue veins behind her wrists, in her throat, deep inside her body.

'I thought you'd gone back to the States,' she said huskily, sitting up.

'As you see, I haven't,' he returned with dry derision.

'Kit isn't here; he and Janet have gone to the beach.'

'I didn't come to see Kit.'

She had been afraid of that; she swallowed and looked down to hide her nervous apprehension.

'I came to see you,' he added, but far from pleasantly, his tone was a threat and she braced herself to meet whatever was coming.

'What about?'

'I gather this guy Molyneaux is a permanent fixture in your life,' he began, and she bristled, guessing that he had been picking up gossip about herself and Ziggy which would probably paint their relationship in pretty lurid colours.

'Who says?' she challenged, frowning.

'Kit,' he said drily, and she bit her lip.

'Kit?' Taken aback, she stared at him, wondering what else Kit had said, then her temper soared. 'You've been interrogating him about my private life? How could you stoop so low? I might have known; you're capable of anything, but what a despicable thing to do, getting Kit to tell you things like that!'

'I did nothing of the kind,' Logan bit out angrily, a dark red invading his face. 'I never ask about you! I never mention you to him.'

Christie didn't like that much, either; it was irrational after accusing him of questioning their son about her to resent the fact that he never talked about her at all, but she didn't stop to unravel her own tangled reactions, she simply simmered with fury, glaring at him. He was looming over her, very tall and powerful in a pale blue lightweight suit and shirt in a deeper blue which he wore open at the throat, without a tie. He looked casual; yet the effect he had wasn't casual. Being around Logan was like sitting on top of a pile of dynamite; Christie felt she might get caught in an explosion any minute. When she was with Ziggy it was like drifting, light as thistledown, in sunny summery air. Logan was storm and whirlwind; his grey eyes had the impervious metallic glitter of steel, emphasised by the smooth tan of his skin around them.

She pretended to laugh disbelievingly. 'I see, he just happened to bring the subject up.'

'That's exactly what happened,' Logan said curtly. 'He talks a blue streak in between firing off questions of his own and yesterday this guy

Molyneaux seemed to be on his mind, he never stopped talking about him. I merely listened.'

'And drew conclusions of your own, I suppose!'

'Naturally. I'm human.'

'You kid yourself,' said Christie, and felt him tense, drawing a fierce breath. The prickle of the hair on the back of her neck warned her not to provoke him further; his eyes gave the same advice. She slid off the lounger and stood up. It might be wiser to terminate this discussion before they both lost their tempers.

'Anyway, my relationship with Ziggy is no business of yours. We're divorced, remember? I haven't even seen you for years—you aren't walking in now and putting me through a quiz about one of my friends!'

She moved sideways to pass him and go into the villa, and Logan's hand shot out to grasp her wrist.

'I don't give a damn who you're sleeping with . . .' he began, and she felt that buzz of fury again; her ears were deafened by it.

'Thank you!' she almost shouted at him. 'That's very broad-minded of you—I've got carte blanche, have I?'

His eyes narrowed, his expression altered and Christie could have kicked herself for losing her temper; she knew she was flushing, and tried to pull herself free, but Logan's fingers tightened.

'Would you rather I minded?' he asked oddly, very softly, watching her with an intent observation that made her look away.

She stared at the villa wall and saw a tiny green lizard dart from a cluster of ivy and halt; throat pulsing, it stared around with a moist fixed eye, then shot out of sight again under an ivy leaf. Christie tried to pull herself together; it was absurd to be so disturbed, nothing had happened, nothing had changed, the tremors of fear running through her had no real cause, yet she felt like some hapless insect on that sunlit wall, stalked by the silent predator behind the sway of green ivy. She was nervous and intensely aware of the man beside her; his cool fingers pressed on her veined wrist as though he was checking the rapid beat of her pulse and she didn't want him to know the effect he was having on her.

'Your opinion is a matter of total indifference to me,' she managed at last in a calm, clear voice. 'I don't know what you're implying, but Kit's very fond of Ziggy, they get on very well, they always have, and Ziggy loves Kit. There's never been any trouble between them.' She looked round at him again and her breath caught in her throat; his hair in the sunlight had the gleam of a blackbird's wing and the lean body so close to her the savage elegance of the jungle, a power made beautiful by the smooth co-ordination of muscle and bone under that golden skin.

He was still watching her in that silent intensity—she was drawn inward by that gaze, sucked into the maelstrom of the black pupils, drowning, breathless, unable to save herself and yet unable to guess what he was thinking, not even knowing what she thought herself, only what she felt, a chaotic jumble of emotions. He was as dangerous as midnight, and she flinched from him.

'Why are you so nervous?' he murmured with a mockery his smile underlined.

'I'm not!'

'Liar,' he said, and his hand slid up her bare arm; his skin familiar, troubling, making her tremble, so sensitive to that touch that her heart rammed against her ribs, as if it meant to smash through them, batter her to shreds. His fingers made her too aware of her own flesh, their caress was already beginning to build up a sensual urgency inside her; her throat raw with sexual longing, heat between her thighs, awaking too many memories of languorous summer afternoons in a warm bedroom with the blinds closed or long, dark nights of gentleness and desire. She had been too innocent then to know how passion could burn and melt the flesh; she had loved without knowing love, yielded to the imperative hands without understanding what made them shake. Eager and excited as a child with a new toy, how could she guess love was sharp and glittering as a knife? Only when she had learnt to cry, bled, run away, did she begin to understand, and to fear love.

'You're even more beautiful now than you were when I first met you,' Logan whispered, his hand on her shoulder. 'You were almost skinny then; you have a few new curves that suit you. That's a great tan you have, too—are you that colour all over?'

Before she could answer his fingers tugged at the strings tying her bikini, and Christie gave an angry wail as the tiny piece of black cloth fell away. She grabbed for it, stepping back from him, her face deeply flushed. Logan was staring at the exposed flesh; nascent, smooth, untouched by the sun.

Christie did not follow the Riviera fashion of
going topless, you never knew when photographers
would sneak up and take a picture of you. She
fumbled with the straps and tied them firmly, her
back to him.

'You'd better go before I lose my temper,' she
said fiercely.

'Why the fuss? I've seen you naked before.'

He was amused; she heard the mockery in his
drawling voice and it made her even angrier.

'The fact that we were married once doesn't give
you the right to . . . to . . .' she stammered into
silence, confused, not knowing how to end that
sentence, and Logan laughed softly.

'To what? Take your clothes off?'

'No,' she muttered, hating him. 'It doesn't. Just
keep your hands to yourself in future!'

'Why the scene? If I go down to Cannes I'll see
dozens of girls sunbathing topless.'

'That's their affair. I never go topless.'

'So I noticed,' he murmured, and her flush
deepened at the reminder that he had seen her pale
breasts, their skin untouched by the sun. 'Have
you ever been asked to do a nude scene in a film?'
he asked as though curious. 'I suppose you'd
refuse?'

'Yes, I would, and I have,' she snapped.
Swinging round, she looked at him with scathing
dislike. She must have been out of her mind to feel
that intense sexual awareness a moment ago. It
had taken her by surprise, she hadn't expected it;
she had never felt anything like that with anyone,
looking back at the years of their marriage she
knew that even Logan had never got to her like

that before. She had been too young, too inexperienced, at eighteen to understand the magnetic force of her own sexuality, the mesmeric lure of the senses. At that age love had all been in the head; the body's demands hadn't begun. She wasn't an unawakened young girl any more, though, she was a woman, and she had wanted Logan with all a woman's sensuality.

'I still don't know what you're doing here,' she said. 'I like Ziggy and so does Kit—but that's nothing to do with you.'

'I didn't say Kit didn't like him, but I don't want my son spending so much time with someone like Molyneaux,' Logan said, and Christie lost her temper.

'He could do a lot worse!' she almost snarled, and Logan arched his brows.

'I doubt that.'

'He could spend too much time with you,' Christie threw at him. 'I wouldn't wish that on any child!'

Logan's mouth hardened and his smile went. 'That's a pretty vicious thing to say! You've made sure I don't see much of him, haven't you? I haven't interfered before because Kit was so young, but once he starts taking notice of what's going on around him he'll need a father.'

'Then maybe I'd better find him one,' snapped Christie.

Logan watched her, narrow-eyed. 'So now we get to the point,' he said with each word bitten out clearly.

'Well, I'm glad to hear it, I wondered if we ever would.' Christie folded her arms, her body posed casually. 'So what is it?'

'Kit has a father. Me. I'll never agree to any other man taking my place.'

Christie was proud of her acting ability; she laughed almost spontaneously. 'No court would give you custody of Kit and you know it. I've looked after my son since he was born and I'd never let you have him. Before you could get custody you'd have to prove that I wasn't looking after him properly. Are you seriously expecting to convince anyone of that? They'd only have to come here, see him, spend ten minutes with him, to know he was a happy little boy who was loved and well looked after.'

'At the moment,' Logan agreed shortly.

'He always will be!'

'Ziggy Molyneaux's not the sort of man I want bringing up my son,' Logan told her. 'Kit's afraid you're going to marry him.'

Taken by surprise, Christie stared at him.

Logan nodded. 'Kit isn't too happy about that; he told me Uncle Ziggy was okay, but he doesn't want a new daddy.'

Christie was too shaken to say anything; she couldn't believe that Kit had thought about it, had guessed that she might marry Ziggy. He had known Ziggy most of his life, he seemed so fond of him, he hadn't given her any indication that he resented the man's constant presence.

'I don't believe you,' she said slowly after a minute. 'Kit would have said something to me.'

'Not if he's jealous of Molyneaux,' said Logan with a shrug, and smiled at her widening eyes. 'Surely that had occurred to you? Children are possessive; they can't help it, their mother is their security blanket, they cling to her for their lives and when a man is always around, claiming her attention, taking it from them, they feel threatened. It's worse with Kit. You're all he has; you've locked me out of his life. Now you're trying to put some other man in my place. Of course Kit resents it.'

'You're putting your thoughts into his head,' Christie accused impatiently. 'It's you that . . .' she broke off, biting her lip and Logan's mouth twisted.

'Me that's jealous of Molyneaux? Is that what you were going to say? No, Christie, I'm just defending my son. He doesn't want you to marry the guy. He told me . . . he doesn't want another daddy. That's good enough for me. So I warn you—if you plan to marry again, you're going to have to fight me for custody of Kit, because I'm not going to stand aside and let some other man play father to my son!'

He turned and walked away; his black shadow kept pace with him on the sunlit path. She heard his car door slam and the engine start, then he drove away and Christie slowly walked into the villa. The maid was busy vacuuming; the whine of the machine sounded oddly loud in the quiet rooms. Christie went upstairs and showered, put on pink jeans and a white shirt, and began to brush her hair. The light, silvery strands were damp and curled as she brushed them.

She heard Janet's voice downstairs, a few moments later, then the clatter of Kit's feet on the stairs. He burst into the room, his dark hair dishevelled.

'You should have come, we had a great time. I swam and I had an ice-cream and Janet nearly went to sleep!'

Christie smiled, watching his face searchingly. He looked so excited and happy; his skin flushed and bloomed with salt, his eyes bright. He didn't look like a child worrying about anything. Had Logan told her the truth? Had Kit told his father that he did not want her to marry Ziggy?

'Is Ziggy back yet?' she asked, alert to every flicker of expression in his small face.

'No, I don't think so, shall I go and see?' Kit rushed off, calling, 'Ziggy, Ziggy!' She heard him tap on Ziggy's bedroom door, open it, then he was back, shaking his head. 'No, he isn't there.' There was no shadow in his eyes, no hint of hidden resentment or jealousy. Logan was imagining it, Christie decided, or deliberately misreading something Kit had said, and her mouth tightened. Logan had worried her and now she was angry. She was going to take Kit to London as soon as possible; she was disturbed by Logan's last remark. It had been a cool threat and she wasn't going to give Logan a chance of putting that threat into action. Once she and Kit were in England, Logan wouldn't be able to part them. In future when he wanted to see his son, she was going to make certain that there was always someone else present. She didn't trust Logan.

CHAPTER FIVE

THEY flew to London two days later, running the usual gauntlet of pressmen at Nice airport. Most of the world's press sent a team to cover the Cannes Film Festival; and as the exodus of stars began there was always a crowd of journalists and cameramen hanging around the crowded airport foyer waiting for famous faces. Christie expected it, she sent Janet on ahead with Kit before she left the limousine bringing them to the airport. Christie took great care to keep her son out of the limelight, and as Ziggy was travelling with them she did not want Kit to overhear any of the questions that got asked.

'Christie, will you be seeing Bud soon?' asked one reporter, and she smiled sweetly at him.

'Bud who? I don't know any Bud.'

The press laughed. A young girl in a white suit asked her: 'What are your plans now? Is there a new film?'

Someone else asked at the same time: 'Seen Carol Heaven lately?' and someone from the back shouted: 'What do you wear in bed, Christie?' A reporter jostling for a place, asked: 'Is Ziggy writing the music for your new film?'

'What new film?' asked Christie, and before they could pelt her with any more questions said: 'My immediate plans are to do some work in the theatre, I'm not planning to make a film for a while. I'm going to London to talk to people about a play I might do.' She smiled around the pushing circle of faces. 'That's all I have to say, gentlemen and ladies.' She turned to move off, with Ziggy close beside her, and the babble of questions followed them.

'What was the fight in the Casino about?'

'Do you and Ziggy plan to marry?'

'Christie, are you happy with the way your film was received at the Festival?'

'Christie, can't we have one more picture with you and Ziggy?'

'Ziggy, why did you hit Bud?'

'Is it true you've been living together for years?'

When they finally escaped their pursuers they made their way to the V.I.P. waiting-room and Christie sank down on one of the chairs with a sigh of relief. Janet was reading a magazine while she drank some coffee, Kit was charging around making aeroplane noises and waggling his arms, occasionally landing to sip some orange juice before taking off again. The uniformed girl in attendance brought Ziggy and Christie some coffee after they had refused, with groans, the champagne she first offered.

'At this time of day? No, thanks,' said Ziggy, and Christie said: 'Champagne would give me a headache; I only drink it at dinner.'

Ziggy sipped his black coffee, eyes closed. 'I'm dead! Next year I'll give the festival a miss. I've lost count of the films I've seen and I only enjoyed a couple of them.' He grinned, opening his eyes. 'By a strange coincidence they were the films I'd scored, and my music was the best thing in them.'

'How amazing,' Christie mocked, laughing. 'I hope mine was one of them.'

'Of course.'

'It was all the parties and receptions I hated,' she said. 'You have to go, you're there to be seen, but it can be exhausting. My teeth hurt from smiling.'

'Mine ache from being ground together. The lies I've told! The compliments I didn't mean! I was ashamed to listen to myself.'

Christie watched Kit as he flew past, long-legged and skinny in chocolate velvet cord pants and a cherry red shirt. A fierce ache of love filled her; he was so young and vulnerable and she couldn't bear to think of anyone or anything hurting him. She knew he was working off energy; for the next couple of hours he would have to sit still in a seat in the plane and he was running while he could, like most children Kit hated to sit still for long.

Ziggy lowered his voice. 'When are we going to announce that we're getting married?'

'I don't know, Ziggy, I can't think about it yet, I'm not sure it . . . you see, I'm worried . . . oh, I don't know.'

He frowned at her low, stammered words. 'What's wrong? You're not going to change your mind, are you? Christie, it will be okay, believe me, don't get cold feet now.'

She glanced sideways at his face; it was tense and pale. His blue eyes held a pleading that upset her even more.

'Don't pressure me, Ziggy—give me time to think it out properly, there's so much to take into account. I don't know how Kit would take it.'

'Kit and I get on like a house on fire, you know that!' He frowned. 'Don't use Kit as an excuse, Christie, because that won't wash.' In pursuit of what he wanted Ziggy was tenacious, like most human beings; she saw the frustrated urgency in his face and felt guilty again. She was fond enough of him to want to give him what he wanted so badly, but she knew her affection wasn't deep enough or strong enough as a response to how Ziggy felt towards her. Even without Logan's intervention she would have been having second thoughts about her promise to marry Ziggy; her own common sense told her that she was taking a risk if she went ahead with it, she didn't need Logan to warn her about that.

They were whispering because there were other people around. Christie sometimes felt she lived her whole life in public, she had to watch every word she said, everything she did, it was tiring and she was sick of it.

'You need someone to look after you—let me do it,' Ziggy whispered, his hand on hers.

Before she could answer, Kit landed on her lap, snuggling up with his head on her shoulder. He turned his face up to her and she kissed the tip of his nose.

'Having fun?'

'I just thought,' Kit announced, 'what about my toys? We left them all at home. I want them.'

'They've been packed up and they'll be arriving in England soon,' Christie said quickly. 'Don't worry, we haven't left anything behind, all your things will be sent on, but it may take a few weeks.' Before Kit could press her, she said:

'Tomorrow we'll go and see Grandma and Grandpa—won't that be nice? They've got a dog; you can play with him.'

'How big is he?' Kit asked warily; he was still a little nervous of big dogs.

'Not very big,' said Christie. 'He's a spaniel.'

'What's that?'

'He has big floppy ears and a bushy tail, and he's called Dandy.' She smiled down at his thoughtful expression. 'He's a goldy colour with white patches on his face. You'll like him. He's the same age as you.'

Their flight was called and she stood up, putting Kit down and taking his hand. As he trotted beside her across the room he talked about the dog, asking more questions. When they boarded the plane Kit sat beside her and went on talking about Dandy, his interest surprising her into asking him: 'Would you like a dog?'

Kit hesitated. 'A little dog,' he suggested in that wary tone.

'We'll get a puppy. You can choose him yourself, once we've found somewhere else to live.'

Kit turned round in his seat, kneeling up, to tell Janet loudly. Other passengers listened, smiling as he gabbled: 'Mummy's going to get me a dog—a little one, a puppy! I'm going to choose him myself.'

'What a lovely idea!'

Christie looked round, meeting Janet's eyes. 'More work for you, I'm afraid, will it be too much?'

'I love dogs! It won't bother me at all, in fact it will be fun. We should have thought of it before, good company for Kit.' Janet was always so calm and reasonable, she took everything in her stride. Christie didn't know what she would do without her. She had made it so easy to cope with the problem of Kit. When you had a child you were presenting yourself with built-in problems on too many levels; practical, emotional, financial. Janet had taken care of all the practical problems. Christie's film earnings had made it unnecessary to worry about the money side of it. But only Christie herself could deal with the emotional results of having Kit, and she worried about her own inadequacy faced with the child's need for love. Oh, she loved Kit, and she was sure he knew it, but Logan had put so many doubts into her head.

How could you help but question yourself, your own motives, your own behaviour, when you knew that what you did affected another human being so deeply? That was why she hadn't wanted a child in the first place—she had known, instinctively, that it would be a full-time emotional drain, and she had been so ambitious. It hadn't been fame she was hunting—it had been a self-fulfilment, the excitement of stretching herself and finding out about herself, the fascination of assuming someone else's life and character for a while with all that that could teach about oneself. She had been afraid that a child would hold her back; take up too much of her.

Perhaps she had felt the same way about Logan; that hadn't occurred to her. Had she secretly resented him once she realised that loving him consumed so much of her emotional energy? She had been too young, they had met at the wrong time. She had been starting out on a road her instincts led her to choose and Logan had tried to deflect her from that path; that was why she had felt so bitter. She had been wrenched, torn one way and then another, with Logan trying to force her to choose him instead of her career and something inside her urging her to choose her career if she was ever to be truly herself. She had been violently angry with him because of the intolerable nature of that forced choice.

During the short flight she listened attentively to Kit, watching for some hint of hostility to Ziggy, but noticing nothing that betrayed jealousy or anxiety. Had Logan lied? Or jumped to conclusions he wanted to be true? Kit talked excitedly about Ziggy's promise to take him that week to London Zoo to see the monkey and lions and have a ride on a camel.

'Daddy has a picture of him riding on a camel,' he told her. 'In the desert; Daddy fell off.' He giggled. 'He slid down the camel's neck and fell on the sand. And I bet it hurt! I won't fall off. I rode on a donkey, didn't I? And I didn't fall off. Do you remember me riding on a donkey, Mummy?'

The stewardess brought him a tray of food and Christie helped him peel off the cellophane wrapping. Kit wrinkled his nose over the lobster salad and the pâté; he nibbled the cheese and ate some of the fruit. Christie just had black coffee and some orange juice. She had no appetite today, especially for the cold, plastic food which Kit was pushing around in distaste.

She was relieved when they got through the

Heathrow formalities quickly and drove off in a limousine towards the centre of London, the boot piled with their cases. The majority of her clothes would be arriving with the rest of their possessions some weeks later, but she had taken quite a few cases to the South of France.

They were installed in a spacious suite in a hotel close to Park Lane; high up with a view over the rooftops and green trees of Hyde Park. Janet took Kit off to rest for an hour while she unpacked his case and her own. Christie lay down on the couch and watched television for a while before she fell asleep without noticing it. It was a raw chill day in London; the green leaves on the trees shivered and the sky had a damp mist stealing through it. It was hard to believe that only that morning when they left Nice they had been under blue skies and hot sunshine.

Christie was woken by the shrilling of the phone. It was the hotel receptionist; her London agent had arrived to see her. Christie told the girl to send him up, then she rang Room Service and ordered drinks and some sandwiches. She was suddenly hungry.

Her agent was a charming man when you were successful; Christie had heard that he wasn't quite so delightful if you didn't make it, but so far she hadn't had to find out. He made a big thing of kissing her hand, as though coming straight from France she might have become used to that.

'You look marvellous, darling,' he flattered, and she didn't bother to tell him that after he had been announced she had rushed into the bathroom to restore her usual immaculate looks, after her short sleep had left her dishevelled and flushed. If he had seen her ten minutes ago!

He sat down and looked around. 'Nice!' he commented. 'Are you serious about staying? Have you considered . . .'

'I'm serious, I won't change my mind,' said Christie. 'I want to do some work in the theatre and it has to be London. While I'm waiting for you to find me something, I shall look for a house somewhere central.'

Roger sighed. He was a short man, sturdy and ruddy-fleshed with a smile that came a little too readily and had no depth. His brown hair was thick and glossy, his voice creamy, his brown eyes small and birdlike and sharp. Christie wasn't sure how old he was; he looked after himself and dressed well, he could be any age between forty and sixty.

'I'm not going to look for a part for you,' he told her. 'We don't want people to think you're available; it puts them off. Just be seen around. You know the style—nightclubs, dancing, parties. If you're asked, say you're considering offers but don't be drawn on any of them. We'll see what fish come to the bait.'

Room Service arrived with the drinks and sandwiches. Roger accepted some whisky but refused the food. He stayed another ten minutes, discussing her latest film, asked after Ziggy, chuckled over the fight in the Casino. 'Great picture, darling; saw it everywhere!' and then departed with every appearance of reluctance, leaving Christie well aware that he had stayed exactly as long as he had planned to stay, not a

second less, not a second more. Roger was a
master of timing. She could learn a lot from him
about that subject; it was one of the most vital
secrets of acting. Roger had been an actor before
he became an agent. He had failed miserably in the
theatre because he had no sex appeal, no stage
presence and no interest in playing the part of
anyone but himself. Roger hadn't failed because
he couldn't act, though. He could act with utter
conviction; but only in one part. He played himself
perfectly.

Kit woke up, pink and cheerful, had some tea
and clamoured to go out. It was early evening by
then, London was in the middle of the rush hour,
the shops were closing and so were all the
museums and galleries. Janet and Christie took
Kit on a walk and then managed to get a taxi to
show them something of the busy city. Kit was not
very impressed, he stared out at the shops and
grey buildings, brooding. 'I wish there was a
beach,' he said. Kit had a one-track mind.

That night Christie dreamt that she ran naked
through flying foam on a sunlit beach, laughing,
and Logan suddenly stood there, a peach in his
hand. She felt shy and nervous, and Logan stroked
the golden fruit for a moment, watching her, then
handed it to her and she bit into it; through the
furry outer skin to the luscious flesh, the juice
trickling down her chin. Logan drew her down on
to the sand and his hard, tanned body was naked
too. It arched over her and she cried out with an
anguished desire and woke up, sweating and
shaking, and for a moment couldn't remember
where she was, and stared around the hotel

blankly. It had never happened. She would never have thought of going on the beach naked, yet her heart thudded as though it had been real. She lay staring at the solid, impervious objects in the room, fighting to regain control. Why on earth had she dreamt that? She still felt the burning need, the frustration ached in her body. She drank some water and forced herself to go back to sleep and this time not to dream.

She took Kit to visit her parents next day. They lived in a small frame house, painted white, on the edge of Epping Forest not far from the centre of London and yet right in the middle of the countryside. The forest was hundreds of years old; it had been planted by the Normans, and Christie had loved to ride through it on her stolid Welsh pony when she was a child; under the towering beech trees and gnarled hornbeams, among the flickering shadows, in and out of sunlit glades. The atmosphere was haunted; the dark moist earth rich with centuries of leafmould which gave the air a graveyard scent. Legend had it that Boadicea had slept there on the night before her last battle with the Romans; at Ambersbury Banks, then an Iron Age fort of grassy mounds, now totally swallowed up in the later forest. Christie had loved to imagine she saw campfires gleaming among the trees, heard the clash of arms, the uncomforted cry of women. She told Kit the old story and although he had never heard of Boadicea he was fascinated, too, perhaps because the legend ended with a battle; a victory and a defeat. Like most boys, Kit was excited by war.

When a journalist asked Christie why she had

wanted to be an actress she could never think of
an answer; it seemed such a stupid question—how
did anyone know why they went along one path
rather than another? From her very earliest years
she had longed to act; she couldn't remember a
time when she had wanted to do anything else, but
her mother had done a lot of amateur acting; that
probably had something to do with it. Christie had
started to see plays when she was very small, her
feet hadn't even touched the floor as she perched,
totally absorbed, on a front seat in the local hall.
She could remember many of those productions;
her mother had always had a leading role. She was
one of the 'stars' of the amateur company. Christie
had once asked her why she hadn't tried to act
professionally and her mother had laughed,
shaking her head, and said she had never been
good enough. Christie could remember her own
disbelief and amazement. She had thought her
mother was the best actress in the world.

It was her mother who opened the front door,
her face lighting up. 'Aren't you both brown?
Come in; it's going to rain again any minute.'
Inside the tiny hall she hugged Kit, picked him up
and said: 'What long legs—you're going to be tall,
aren't you?'

Kit thought about that. 'Yes,' he decided, and
Christie and her mother laughed. They were very
alike, it had been from Delia Mottram that
Christie had inherited her fine silvery hair and
blue eyes, her pale skin and slight figure. Delia's
hair had turned totally silver now; it shone like
filigree platinum. Her eyes had faded in colour,
her face was even thinner but she had great

style; she moved and dressed like a woman of thirty, with elegance and an instinctive sense of what suited her. She had a deeper voice than Christie, however; it sounded odd to hear that rounded, full tone coming from her slender body, and she used her voice to give each word she uttered a clarity and music that made it a pleasure to listen to her.

'Where's Dad?' Christie asked, and her mother smiled at her.

'In the kitchen, taking off his muddy boots. He took the day off work to see you and he's been in the garden all morning.'

The kitchen door opened and Gerald Mottram appeared in a shaggy brown cardigan and his old gardening trousers. He held out his arms and she ran to hug him, thinking: he's getting old! It made her feel like crying, but she smiled as she looked at his thinning brown hair and wrinkled forehead, the betraying stoop of his thin body.

'It's much too long since I saw you—are you well? You look wonderful,' she lied, hoping he wasn't ill, it was only age catching up with him. He was nearly sixty and no doubt he had grown older gradually, it was just that she hadn't seen him for ages, she was realising all at once that he was no longer a youngish man. Her mother was managing to stay young in looks, but she wasn't more than two years off sixty, although you'd never guess it.

'Would you like some milk and a biscuit?' Delia asked Kit, who shook his head. He was busy staring at a dog which had wandered in from the kitchen and was licking Christie's hands while she fondled his silky coat. Dandy was very well behaved; although his tail wagged furiously he didn't bark.

Delia put Kit down, holding his hand. 'Say hello to Dandy,' she invited, and Kit tentatively stroked the spaniel. Christie held her breath, hoping Dandy wouldn't alarm him, but the dog behaved beautifully and Kit was beginning to laugh with excitement.

'Like some coffee?' her mother asked her, and she nodded, following Delia into the kitchen.

'Oh, you've redecorated!' she exclaimed, halting.

Her mother looked around the room, frowning. 'Oh, that was two years ago,' she said. 'I was just beginning to think we ought to do it again. Kitchen walls take such a beating—all that steam.' She put the kettle on the electric hob. 'Instant coffee, okay?'

'That's fine,' said Christie, going over to the window to stare at the garden. It was another misty day; the trees dripped dejectedly and the tulips and white lilac flowering in the garden couldn't compete with the greyness of the weather. There was an apple tree in bloom, sprays of delicate pinky white blossom. Behind the garden fence she saw the massing trees of the forest; their leaves new-minted, vivid, but coils of mist blowing along the damp paths.

'We've been reading the reviews of your new film. It seems to have been well received, are you pleased with it?' Delia put out a row of cups on the well-scrubbed deal table at which Christie could remember doing her homework years ago. It had more scars on it now; knife cuts where her mother had sliced bread, an ink stain from long ago.

Christie talked about the film, sitting down to watch her mother making the coffee. 'How's Ziggy?' asked Delia after she had called her husband.

'He's fine, he's in London this week—he goes back to the States to start work on his next score soon.'

Her father came in, Kit trotting behind him alongside the spaniel. The two of them curled up on the rug in front of the electric fire which the unseasonable weather demanded, and Gerald Mottram sat down opposite Christie. They had always used the kitchen in preference to the long room which acted both as a dining-room and a sitting-room; that was less cosy, a place for guests. The kitchen had always been the heart of the house, that was where Delia was most of the time, cooking and preserving fruit, making jams and pickles, sewing and ironing, washing and just sitting in front of the fire reading her latest part or a book.

'Any news of a job yet?' her mother asked, offering her a plate of home-made wafer-thin chocolate shortcake.

Christie took one and bit into it blissfully; they had always been her favourite biscuits; she knew her mother had made them specially. 'Delicious as always,' she said, and Delia laughed, looking pleased. 'Not yet,' Christie went on. 'But then it always takes time and I haven't worked in the theatre for years. I've only done one professional job in the States. Managements won't take my film work into account. I'll have to go through the same mill as everybody else. I'll have to prove I can act before anyone will take me seriously over here, you know that.'

'It's an overcrowded profession,' Gerald Mottram said soberly. 'Christie, are you wise to take a risk like this? Your mother is all for it, but I'm not so sure. You're doing so well in films, and wasn't there talk of a TV serial? Why throw all that groundwork away?'

'I have to,' Christie said wryly. 'Don't ask me why, Dad. Do you think I haven't had dark warnings from everyone around me? I know I'm being reckless, but I didn't go into acting to work in films, I wanted to go on the stage—I still do, and for the next year I can afford to rest on my laurels and wait for offers.'

'Christie's quite right,' said Delia. 'She isn't going anywhere in films; she's a born stage actress, it would be a crime to waste that talent. She has to follow her own instincts.'

'So long as she isn't following yours,' Gerald said gently. 'I know you always dreamt she would go on the stage, but Christie can't live her life for you and you can't live through her, either.'

'I'm not trying to,' Delia protested, looking angry. She looked at Christie. 'Have I ever tried to push you into a stage career? Have I?'

'Of course not,' said Christie, surprised and disturbed by the argument between her parents. She could remember them quarrelling occasionally when she was small, but in recent years they had rarely argued and she didn't want them to do so over her. 'Nobody had to push me, Dad—I never wanted to do anything else. Maybe I did get the bug from Mum, but not because she *tried* to influence me. In fact, I remember her warning me about all the drawbacks. She almost tried to talk me out of it.' She smiled at her mother. 'Didn't you now? Gave me a real gypsy's warning.'

'I didn't want you to go ahead without knowing the risks,' said Delia, smiling back. 'It's the toughest profession in the world.'

'So it was unconscious,' Gerald Mottram said. 'Your mother didn't know she was nudging you all the time, but deep down she dreamt of nothing else. Oh, come on now, Delia—didn't you want Christie to be what you'd never managed to be? Whether you pushed her or not, it was your dream she was living out.'

Her mother seemed uncertain, she looked at Christie and then at Gerald Mottram, knitting her brows. 'I don't think so—I was contented with my amateur status.' She forced a laugh. 'It was a lot less of a strain. You know the stomach cramps I get when I'm going on stage, think how I'd have been if I'd been a professional! You need drive and determination to make it in the real theatre and I didn't have either, but I don't think I tried to influence Christie, not knowingly, anyway.'

'It doesn't seem to me to matter, in any case,' Christie said impatiently. 'The fact is, I've always wanted to be an actress. What difference does it make now whether Mum wanted it too, or it was all my own idea?'

Her father lowered his voice. 'If it hadn't been for your obsession with acting, your marriage might have worked out.'

Christie paled, glancing round at Kit, who was still playing with the dog. He grinned as she caught his eye and got up, came over and leant against her knee. 'Mummy's going to buy me a dog,' he told his grandparents. 'A little tiny one. And when I've got my dog Daddy and me will take it for walks. Daddy had a dog; he used to throw sticks in the sea and his dog brought them back.' He paused, looking thoughtful. 'But there's no sea in London so we can't play that, but Daddy will think of a game.'

Christie met her parents' eyes. The spaniel on the rug stirred, got up and padded to the back door, whining to be let out. Kit ran after him into the garden, and Gerald Mottram went with them, closing the door on a wave of clammy mist.

'Does he see much of Logan?' her mother asked.

'Logan visits him when he can.'

'Kit's very fond of him?'

'Yes,' said Christie almost with defiance, as though her mother was hinting at something that felt like criticism.

'If you're in England . . .' began Delia, frowning disapproval.

'I know,' Christie said. 'What am I supposed to do? Stay over there so that Kit can see his father whenever Logan has the time? I love Kit very much, I want him to be happy, but I'm not just his mother, I have my own life to lead. I'm the one who takes care of Kit, not Logan. He visits him maybe once or twice a month for a few hours. Kit's with me every day, he's far more my son than he is Logan's.'

'I know how hard it is for you; I wasn't criticising you.'

'Sometimes I feel I'm being torn in half,' sighed

Christie, watching Kit through the kitchen window as he ran up and down the narrow garden paths, shouting and laughing with the dog on his heels. 'It isn't easy to combine a career with being a mother; something gets sacrificed all the time. I just try to make sure it's never Kit. So long as he's happy and well, I can feel easy, and I think I'll see even more of him when I'm working in the theatre than I can now. I won't have to spend the days in the studio or out on location, I can be with Kit, and he'll go to bed while I'm working in the evenings. I think it will work out beautifully. The only problem is Logan.'

'How did he take the news that you planned to move to London?'

'He doesn't know yet,' Christie said with a little grimace. 'I didn't quite have the nerve to tell him.'

Her mother looked at her sharply. 'Oh, dear,' she said, and Christie nodded. 'I couldn't put it better myself.'

CHAPTER SIX

THE following day Ziggy took Kit to London Zoo, while Christie spent the morning seeing house agents and visiting a lawyer, to check that Logan's threat to fight her for custody of their son was an empty one. Reassured by a bland man in a pinstriped suit, she returned to the hotel and found that Janet was out shopping and Ziggy and Kit hadn't got back yet, so she curled up on the brocade couch in the suite and looked through a sheaf of printed house advertisements. She had told the agents that she wanted a small three-bedroomed house close to central London. With what was either reckless optimism or plain stupidity they had given her the details of a bizarre collection of properties ranging from a mock-Gothic with eight bedrooms to a one-bedroomed flat in a cul-de-sac. Christie didn't see anything she liked; she tore the sheets up and stuffed them into a wastepaper basket, then went over to the phone to start complaining to the agents. Just as she got to it, the phone rang.

'Hallo?' she said, expecting it to be Ziggy explaining why he was late back with Kit. It was almost lunchtime and they were supposed to be lunching at the hotel.

The phone went dead. 'Hallo?' Christie repeated, puzzled, but nobody answered, so with a grimace she hung up, then began dialling the house agents.

She was halfway through her third bitingly sarcastic call when someone tapped on the outer door. Christie rapidly cut short her conversation, put down the phone and ran to the door, expecting again to find Ziggy and Kit, but it was Logan outside the door, and as their eyes met, Christie, on a reflex, began to shut the door in his face.

He leant his whole weight on the panels and the door was forced back, taking her with it. It was too undignified to struggle; she turned and walked away, and heard him coming behind her. Over her shoulder she said coldly: 'Are you following me around the world? How did you know where I was?'

'When I got back to the States I discovered you'd moved out of your beach cottage and the only forwarding address they had there was your London agent's,' Logan said as she turned to face him. He was angry, she saw that at a glance, his whole body was tense and the grey eyes sparked furiously.

'Haven't you got anything better to do than fly around persecuting me?' Christie wasn't going to sit down; she didn't want to encourage him to stay.

'I had to fly to London on business,' he snapped. 'While I'm here I want to know what you're up to—how long are you staying in London?'

She shrugged. 'No idea.'

'Don't try to pull the wool over my eyes!' Logan leant towards her, his voice icy. 'Why have you sold the beach cottage?'

'I was tired of it, I'm sick of beach life.' She gave

him an aggressive stare. 'Not that that is any of your business.'

'You never mentioned it when I saw you in Antibes!'

'That may be because I didn't see what it had to do with you!'

'What you do with your life is your business. What you do with my son's life is mine,' he bit out, vibrating with rage which made his tanned skin darken with hot blood. Today he was wearing a formal dark suit; smoothly tailored and elegant, probably because of the business he said he had come here for, but the man under the expensive clothes was very far from formal. He was angry enough to use a force which Christie both feared and resented; she stepped back from him instinctively, throwing back at him the anger he was showing her.

'I still don't know how you found me!' she said, to distract him.

'I rang your agent,' he muttered. 'And I've been ringing you for the past four hours without getting a reply.' He looked around, frowning. 'Where's Kit, anyway?'

'At the Zoo—he should be back later today.'

Logan looked at his watch. 'When? I've got a plane to catch at two-thirty, I'll have to go soon.'

'They said they'd be back by one, but maybe Ziggy couldn't get a taxi . . .' She stopped talking as Logan's eyes flashed over her, narrowed and violent.

'He's here?' The question was scalding, distasteful, and she flushed. 'You let him go off with Kit? I wouldn't trust that guy to take a dog for a walk, let alone my son—I don't want Kit going around with him, do you hear me?'

'I should think they can hear you out in the street——' Christie began, then stopped as Logan began to walk away from her, She followed uncertainly, but instead of leaving the suite he looked in at the two bedrooms, glanced around and then entered the room she was using. Her silk nightdress was neatly folded at the foot of the bed. Logan opened the wardrobes while she seethed, baffled and indignant.

'What the hell do you think you're doing?'

'Checking,' he drawled, glancing at the clothes hanging in each wardrobe.

'What . . .' she began, but he cut her short.

'I wanted to see if your boy-friend was sharing your room.' He closed the last wardrobe door and turned. Shaking with anger, Christie hit him, but the blow didn't connect. Logan caught her wrist and held it, used it to drag her close to him. Her stomach crawled with a sudden fierce apprehension; their bodies touched and an electric current sparked between them. Logan looked down at her harshly. 'You weren't going to hit me, were you? That would have been a very stupid thing to do,' he said with threat in his voice. Christie suddenly remembered the erotic dream she had had the other night; her skin ran with heated colour and her breathing quickened. Logan watched her and she heard the intake of his breath, as though he was surprised.

'Are you sleeping with him?' he bit out, and she looked up, then, struggling to hide the powerful instincts which had gripped her.

'1 told you before—my private life is none of your business. You'd better go . . .' She tried to pull away and his other arm went round her, his hand in the small of her back, refusing to let her escape. Their eyes quarrelled, then Logan looked at her mouth and to her dismay Christie felt a strange, boneless weakness; her eyes were tired and hot, she couldn't keep them open as his head came down closer. She felt the way she had felt in her dream; she needed to feel his mouth on her own, she wanted him. The hunger was overwhelming, irresistible. When his lips finally touched hers she arched against him, shuddering, and met his kiss with intense passion. Her mind clouded as she surrendered to the driving impulse which it wanted to resist, her arms went round his neck and she felt his arms tighten round her.

Then the phone rang; they almost leapt apart, breathing thickly. Christie's eyes snapped open; she was still so dazed she could hardly see, she fumbled for the phone with a trembling hand. 'Yes?' Her voice sounded unfamiliar, not her own.

'Darling, I'm sorry, we're going to be another hour at least. Kit dragged me all over the bloody Zoo and I've just collapsed in the café, by the time we've got a taxi and driven back it will be way past lunch.' Ziggy sounded far away; she had to force herself to concentrate on what he was saying in a laughing, cheerful voice. 'Kit wants to have a hamburger here, would you mind if we don't get back for lunch with you?'

'Of course not,' she managed to say huskily. 'That's fine.' She forced a brittle laughter. 'It sounds as if Kit's having a wonderful time.'

'You bet,' said Ziggy, chuckling. 'I don't think there's a spider he hasn't seen; he wouldn't let me leave out a single living creature in this place. I didn't mind the animals so much; it was the reptiles that gave me the creeps. Snakes make my skin crawl and I didn't like the way the alligators looked at me, either. I had the feeling they were thinking about lunching off me.'

Logan was standing behind her, she could hear his breathing, he shifted and her body registered the tiny movement with a leap of the pulses.

'Well, enjoy your hamburger,' she said lightly, and Ziggy said he'd try but his stomach would never forgive him, then he rang off, and Christie turned and looked at Logan, then looked away because she was still trembling and she didn't want him to know.

'They won't be back until much later,' she stammered.

'I'll have to go.' Logan looked at his watch and she stared at his profile with an aching awareness. 'I'll see Kit another time. How much longer are you staying in London?'

'I'm looking at offers here,' she said, and Logan gave her a sharp look.

'A new film? They're going to shoot on location, are they? Or is it being made entirely in England?'

'I don't know yet,' she said, evasively, because she was too strung up to face another row with him. If she told him she meant to move to England for good Logan would miss his plane and stay to argue. He might even begin that custody suit. She had to lie to him.

'But you'll be coming back to California before you start filming?'

Christie hesitated, then nodded.

'Give me a ring when you get back, then.' Logan sounded almost uncertain, he looked at her and smiled, and her heart flopped like a stranded fish.

He looked away and began to walk out of the suite with Christie following him. At the door he paused and without looking at her said quietly: 'I wish I didn't have to get this plane, I think we should talk, but it can wait. Kiss Kit for me.'

'Yes, have a safe flight,' she said with an inner misery that sounded in her voice.

Logan turned, kissed her hard, briefly, then was gone, and she shut the door and leaned on it struggling with tears. She felt like someone in a high-speed train, seeing buildings, faces, fields, rush by at a tremendous rate, dazzling with sharp but brief impressions. That was how Logan made her feel; too much was happening to her when she was with him. She couldn't relate the man she remembered to the man she was meeting now. He had changed. She had changed. The situation between them had changed. One minute she thought one thing; the next she thought something quite different. And in between, she *felt*; with such stabbing and immediate clarity, as though white light pierced her eyeballs illuminating everything, for a flash of time. Then darkness fell again and she groped in it, bewildered.

She looked at herself in the bedroom mirror a moment later. 'What is it you're feeling?' she asked her reflection, and answered with a self-deriding grimace. 'How do I know what I think until I see what I feel?'

Sometimes instinct works better than reason; faster, leaping over proofs and questions, sure of itself without knowing why, but her instincts were working irregularly, clicking on and off at random, and she didn't trust them.

Did Logan know what he was doing, either? Just now, when he kissed her, she had felt his skin burning, heard him breathing jerkily. He had looked at her so strangely just before he left, as though on the point of saying something ... something she had felt would be important, something Logan had thought better of, had caught back and decided not to say.

She locked herself into the bathroom to wash her face; tearstains showed on her cheeks, she didn't want Ziggy or Janet to notice them. While she was in there someone tapped at the outer door of the suite, she went and opened it and Janet gave her a cheerful smile, staggering past under large bags printed with famous names.

'Something tells me you've been shopping,' said Christie.

'I've had a wonderful time. I've spent every cent I had.' Janet let her bags fall on the nearest of the two beds in her own room. 'I could murder a drink and a sandwich—I haven't eaten yet.' She limped, kicking off her shoes, to the phone and dialled Room Service. 'Want anything?'

'Whatever you're having. I haven't eaten either.'

'Beef and salad sandwiches?'

'Sounds fine.' Christie went back to the bathroom to finish brushing her hair. Ten minutes later she and Janet sat down to talk over the drinks and food and by the time they had finished eating Ziggy and Kit had arrived.

'Was the Zoo fun, darling?' Christie asked, and Kit grinned excitedly.

'We saw the sea-lions catch fishes when the man threw them and I had two ice-creams and crisps and a hamburger and . . .'

'Did you go to the Zoo or just to a junk food store?' Christie asked Ziggy.

'He never stops eating, and he almost walked me off my feet. I'm going back to my room to die quietly. See you.' He stopped on the way to ask: 'Come to a party tomorrow night?'

She considered the invitation doubtfully. 'Who's giving it?'

'Theo Nelson.'

Christie looked blank.

'An old buddy of mine,' Ziggy told her. 'He wrote the music for that rock opera, *Moonscape*. I'm sure I took you to see it, don't you remember?'

'Is that the show that gave me a headache for three days afterwards?'

Ziggy laughed. 'That's the one! I thought you'd remember it.'

'Who could forget it?'

'Right. We went on to the first night party. Theo's the guy with the beard and long hair who danced with you a couple of times, I think he rather fancies you.'

'Oh—*him*! I thought he was a St Bernard,' said Christie. 'You mean he writes music? He's a clever dog. When I was a little girl I had a dog that howled to music; I bet it would howl if it heard his.'

Ziggy shook his head indulgently. 'You're in a vicious mood, what's turned your milk sour?'

Christie glanced at Kit, who was peering out of the windows at the busy street below. She did not want to mention his father; it might upset him to know he had narrowly missed seeing Logan. She smiled, shrugging, 'Let's put it down to city life; you need to have your wits sharp to stay alive in this traffic.'

'Well, I'll pick you up at eight,' said Ziggy, and left, and Janet removed Kit to have his daily nap.

Christie spent the next morning with Kit at the Science Museum, pressing buttons and admiring steam engines and early cars and planes. They had lunch at Harrods and Christie bought herself some cashmere cardigans and silk shirts, then they went back to the hotel and had tea in the suite. While Kit was lying down later, Christie had a bath and did her hair and nails before she dressed for the party. From what she recalled of Theo Nelson he wasn't the type to give formal parties. She chose a blue silk catsuit; it was pretty and suited her and it would suit almost any occasion. She decided, staring at herself in the mirror, that she was going to enjoy the evening, she was going to banish Logan from her mind and have some fun. It worried her that she should be spending so much time thinking about a man she had cut out of her life five years ago. It had to stop.

When Ziggy picked her up he halted to stare at her; his eyes running from her drifting silver hair and finely modelled features down over the seductive body in that clinging silk outfit. 'Maybe I shouldn't take you to this party,' he said wryly, rubbing his chin. 'The men will be all round you like bees around a honeypot.'

Christie laughed, her blue eyes teasing him. 'Do you think so?' she queried with mock innocence, and Ziggy eyed her with compunction.

'I don't like that look in your eyes. You're in a mischievous mood.'

'A party mood,' she claimed, linking her hand around his arm. 'You look terrific yourself.' He was wearing black jeans and an open-necked white silk shirt; a wide cream leather belt tight around his slim waist. Ziggy was very good-looking, she thought, as they went down in the lift to the underground car park where he had left his car. He had hired a chauffeur-driven car for the evening so that he could drink at the party. As they drove through the heavy evening traffic Ziggy told her that he had asked the chauffeur to pick them up at one o'clock.

'I know you hate late nights,' he added.

'It isn't late nights I hate—it's being woken up by Kit at eight o'clock in the morning afterwards,' Christie said drily. 'I need my sleep. If I don't have at least seven hours it shows; I start going around with bags under my eyes and I get as snappy as hell.'

Ziggy laughed. 'I wouldn't like that.'

'No, you wouldn't,' she said more soberly. 'I don't like myself when I'm irritable and nor does anybody else, so I always make sure I get my full quota of sleep.'

The party was being held in what looked like a disused warehouse but which Theo Nelson claimed was his studio. It was enormous and bare, but the walls had been hung with vast and violently coloured oil paintings; great blotches of crude colour flung at the canvases. Theo saw her staring at them and said: 'All my own work.'

'Oh, really?' said Christie, taken aback. 'How . . . how marvellous. Aren't you versatile?'

Theo had even more hair than he had had last time she met him. Through the curling mass of it peered blank black eyes. As the evening progressed Christie realised that Theo was stoned out of his mind; he danced with her and tried to persuade her to smoke some of the home-made cigarettes he carried in a tin in his shirt pocket.

'Grass,' she murmured, staring at them and shaking her head. 'I don't use it, thanks. I get high without it.'

Theo looked interested for once. 'How?'

'You ought to try it,' she said wryly. 'I enjoy life.'

Theo began talking in a flat monotone about the wider perception he had acquired, and Christie yawned, looking around for Ziggy. The party was overcrowded with people; few of them were dancing, but they surged around the room drinking and nibbling at strange food which Theo had provided. Christie had decided not to try any of that, either—she had a suspicion it would make her very ill indeed. She didn't like the way Theo's hand was clenching in her silk catsuit, either, or the dull avidity of his eyes on her. He still didn't talk much, but when he did he was boring and often forgot what he had started out to say; his mind wandered and his sentences became incoherent. Christie saw some of the guests lying down in corners, their bodies fitting together like spoons in a drawer. Some were making love, others just sleeping. She looked furtively at her watch on Theo's thin shoulder. It was only midnight, but she felt it was time to go.

The music was being provided by some of Theo's friends; one of them suddenly smashed his guitar over the head of one of the others, who turned, staggering, to swing a punch at the guitarist. A fight started; the dancers crowded arounded to watch, laughing and egging the contestants on. Christie got away from Theo's now openly exploring hands and pushed her way through the throng to find Ziggy.

'Can we go?' she yelled above the din.

Ziggy was lounging against one of the walls, a glass in his hand, talking to a small fluffy-looking girl who stared at Christie curiously.

'Hallo, I'm a big fan of yours,' she said with a feline smile which didn't ring true. She had deepset, slanting brown eyes and a triangular face on which she had brushed too much blusher so that she looked hectic, overheated. Her fairish hair was a light fuzz on top of her head; Christie thought she saw tinsel sprinkled in it but wasn't sure if that was the effect of the spinning lights positioned high above them among the rafters.

'Hallo, nice to meet you,' Christie said automatically.

'This is Dina,' said Ziggy, waving his glass. 'Isn't she cute?'

'Very,' said Christie. The small girl was as cute as a razor; those eyes of hers were so sharp they sliced you.

'Dina's got good taste,' Ziggy announced solemnly. He was slightly drunk, Christie realised, he was being propped up by that wall, he wasn't leaning on it by chance. 'She likes my music.' He grinned. 'Don't you, Dina?'

'Love it,' Dina said, still staring at Christie. 'When are you two getting married, then?'

'Any day now,' Ziggy told her. 'Aren't we, Christie?'

She put an arm around his waist, her mouth tight. 'Come on, let's get out of here.'

Ziggy leant on her, his body surprisingly heavy for someone so slim. Dina took the glass out of his hand and put it down on the floor. 'I'll clear a gangway for you,' she told Christie, and went ahead, pushing people back so that Christie and Ziggy could struggle through to the door. Christie looked at her watch again, wondering if they would have to get a taxi. It was now half-past twelve.

As they emerged into the cold night air Ziggy opened his drowsy eyes. 'Where am I?' He peered at the street lights and the buildings opposite, dazed.

'How do you feel?' asked Christie, steering him and breathing hard.

He lifted his head and looked at her glassily. 'I love you,' he said, and kissed her on the mouth, halting under a street light.

The night was suddenly very bright, Christie pushed him away and looked past to see a man facing them with a camera. Another flashlight went off, and Ziggy laughed.

'Fireworks!'

'Oh, damn,' Christie muttered, her face angry. She should have guessed there would be some press people around at a party like this—there must be nearly two hundred guests, many of them famous names. She looked around desperately at the parked cars in the narrow street—had their limousine come back yet? There were a number of glossy cars waiting, and out of one of them climbed the chauffeur who had driven them here. Christie began propelling Ziggy towards him, desperate to get away before the photographer took any more pictures of him in this state.

The chauffeur took charge of Ziggy and bundled him into the back of the long car, while Christie went round to the other side and climbed in beside him. The doors slammed and the car began to pull out and drive away. Christie glanced back and with a prickle of alarm saw Dina talking to the photographer.

Ziggy sat up, blinking, and gave her a sweet, apologetic smile. 'Sorry, too many gins—sorry, darling.'

'Ziggy, who *is* Dina?'

He looked blank, having trouble keeping his eyes open. 'Who?'

'Dina! The girl you were with just now.'

He half-smiled, a flicker of intelligence in his face. 'Oh, Dina! Pretty little thing—fan of mine, loved the score of *Only Tomorrow*, just saw the film. Works on one of the music papers, gave me a rave write-up . . .'

'A reporter?' asked Christie, aghast.

Ziggy looked worried, petulant. 'What?'

'Ziggy, what did you tell her? What were you

saying to her when I arrived? Ziggy, listen to me . . .'

He didn't answer, he was asleep, his body limply swaying with the movement of the car. She turned to look at him and he fell heavily against her, breathing stertorously. Christie sighed, put an arm around him and held him close, stroking his thick soft hair. He stirred, murmuring happily, and her guilt about him made her tender. She wished she loved him the way he wanted her to, or was that an illusion? Did Ziggy want the sort of love of which she was capable? Or did he want what she already gave him—the same tenderness and protective warmth she felt for her son? The maternal instinct can be a trap, both for those who feel it and for those towards whom it is felt. Women are touched by the weakness of men; it appeals to something deep inside their own psyche, those inherited genes which make a woman hunger for a child. Some men want to be mothered all their lives. Christie's own instincts told her that she would not be happy giving that sort of love to Ziggy for ever. She would be unfulfilled. She had fled from her own awareness of her needs, but she had been made brutally aware of them the last time she saw Logan. Ziggy was all sunshine and sweetness, a loving man who needed to be looked after—Logan was darkness and power, he could hurt her, but she ached for the extremity of passion she would find in his arms.

She had been too young when they first met to understand herself, and without self-knowledge she couldn't match Logan. He had been far ahead of her; her anger and her bitterness were part of the frustration she had felt because she knew she was mishandling their relationship, yet she hadn't been able to stop herself. She had been too driven by ambition, too obsessed with her dream. She couldn't untangle how she felt about Logan from how she felt about the sort of life she wanted. They should have met years later. She had more maturity now, she was less self-obsessed, she understood herself better.

It was ironic that now, when she might be able to cope with Logan, they should be totally divided by all that had happened in the past. She couldn't forgive or forget the violence he had shown her the night he took her by force; there had been no love in that passion, it had been fuelled by hatred and a wish to punish. He had pulled her down into the darkness and it had taken her years to fight her way out of it.

Perhaps it would be wiser to marry Ziggy and give him what she knew she could give him—the loving warmth and companionship which was all she could give. Perhaps that would be enough, after all, for Ziggy, at least. It would mean she wouldn't get hurt again, and all she really knew about the sort of love she had felt for Logan was that in the end it tore you apart. She had had enough of that.

Ziggy woke up when she and the chauffeur helped him out of the limousine. He mumbled an apology, staggering after her into the hotel, and Christie smiled at him. His eyelids looked swollen, his face grey and weary.

'It doesn't matter, it was a party, after all.'

He leaned on the wall of the lift, yawning, a hand to his mouth. 'Was it a good party? I don't remember a thing about it.'

'Not very,' Christie said as the lift stopped; and Ziggy meandered down the carpeted corridor, humming under his breath. He halted outside his room and began hunting for his key. She took it from him when he found it and inserted it, pushed open the door of his room. Ziggy leaned unsteadily towards her and kissed her on the forehead, then he went inside and the door banged. Christie went on to her own suite, her face wry.

She found the suite in darkness. Janet and Kit were fast asleep. She went into the bathroom, undressed, washed, cleansed her face carefully with scrupulous attention to detail and finally fell into bed to sleep like a log.

Janet woke her with a cup of coffee and a piercing stab of daylight as Janet drew the curtains. Christie sat up, yawning, to look at the time. Janet dropped the newspapers on the coverlet. Picking up her coffee, Christie asked: 'Kit okay?'

'He's had his breakfast and is playing with his cars,' Janet said, walking to the door. 'Any plans for the day?' She halted, trim and neat in a rose-pink dress.

'House-hunting. I promised to take Kit to see the dinosaurs in the Natural History Museum some time today; I'll do that this afternoon.'

Janet went out and Christie sipped her coffee, glancing at the newspapers. She came awake with a vengeance as she saw the picture on the front page of one of the popular papers. Her hand trembled and black coffee spilled on the newsprint. She read the story which accompanied the picture, biting her lip. Now she knew what Ziggy had been saying to the girl she found him with last night. Dina had wasted no time in getting her story to the papers. Now the whole world knew that Ziggy and Christie planned to marry soon. Christie winced as she read the quotes from Ziggy.

The phone rang. It was the reception desk. There were reporters downstairs, asking to see her. She told the clerk to say she was out. She did not want to talk to the press, they were to put through no calls to her suite.

She pushed the newspapers away and slid out of bed, put on a silk negligee and went to find Janet. She was with Kit, both of them kneeling on the carpet in the sitting-room, racing a large black toy car. Kit jumped up and kissed Christie who held him tightly, feeling suddenly anxious and vulnerable, and Kit looked up at her uncertainly, sensing her mood. Christie saw his face alter and hurriedly pulled herself together. What was the matter with her? She was worrying Kit.

'It seems to be a nice day, thank goodness—how about a trip on the river?' she suggested.

Kit was delighted with that idea. 'Oh, yes, please!' he exclaimed, jumping up and down, and Janet stared at Christie questioningly.

'I thought you said house-hunting this morning?'

'That can wait. Look at that sunshine—perfect for a trip down to Greenwich.'

Kit bolted off to his own room to hunt for his

outdoor shoes and an anorak. Janet said quietly: 'He didn't see the papers.' Kit couldn't read well, but he would have recognised his mother and the sagging, all too obviously drunken Ziggy she was holding up in that awful picture. Christie sighed, grimacing.

'Thanks,' said Christie. 'Oh, it isn't fair—poor Ziggy, he wasn't that drunk. He doesn't drink that much anyway—it isn't fair, one little slip and there they are, waiting to catch him out. I hate newspapers!' She turned to go into the bathroom, paused and said: 'There are press downstairs. We'll have to sneak out the back way.'

'I'll cope,' Janet said calmly. 'If we spot anyone I'll grab Kit and make a run for it.'

'I don't know what I'd do without you,' Christie told her.

She wore large, owlish dark glasses and a scarf tied over her hair, a belted dark red leather coat with a high collar which helped to hide her face. They got away from the hotel without anyone recognising her. Christie had pushed a note under Ziggy's door, warning him about the press and saying she would be out all day.

The weather was perfect for a river trip; fresh and sunny without being hot. Kit leant on the rail and watched the wake churning behind them, stared at the sights along the river bank which their guide described. He wasn't interested in the history; he liked the water and the novelty of seeing the city from such a new angle. He dutifully stared at Tower Bridge and the Tower itself, at St Paul's and Greenwich Hospital, but what interested him most was the strange objects bobbing along in the slate-blue water, the strings of barges they passed, the anchored ships and the dozens of other fascinating sights he noticed in passage.

They came back by bus to Kensington; had lunch near the Natural History Museum and went on to see the dinosaurs assembled again in the cavernous hall of the museum.

When they returned to the hotel they found a note from Ziggy asking Christie to ring him as soon as she could. She picked up the phone and Ziggy answered the first ring. He was grimly apologetic. 'What can I say? I feel terrible, I'm so sorry, Christie.'

'I forgive you,' she told him. 'There's no point in crying over spilt milk. You haven't talked to anyone else from the press today, I hope?'

'They've been ringing me all day. The hotel told them I was out.'

'That's a relief. Ziggy, I think Kit and I ought to leave London for a few days to let this all blow over. I'm going to take Kit to stay with my parents. I'll give Janet some time off; she deserves a long break.'

Ziggy was silent for a moment. 'I see,' he said at last. 'You're probably wise. I know how you hate the thought of Kit getting caught up in any publicity. I'll be off to the States again in a couple of days. Will I see you before then?'

Gently, Christie said: 'I don't think . . .'

He interrupted. 'Okay, I understand. Christie, I know I was a fool, getting drunk, talking to a reporter—I could cut my tongue out. Don't let this change your mind—I need you.'

'Oh, Ziggy,' she sighed almost inaudibly, her

heart aching. She didn't know how to answer him. Ziggy needed her, but did she need Ziggy? As a dear friend, as someone she loved warmly—but as a man? Her needs could never be answered by Ziggy; that much she was now certain of, but she didn't know how to tell him.

'I'll be in touch,' she said, instead. 'Have a safe flight, good luck with the new job—see you soon.'

She rang off, feeling like an assassin. When they left the suite Janet had stuffed all the daily papers into one of the waste-bins and the maid who cleaned the suite had removed them. There was no remaining sign of Ziggy's folly, but Christie knew she hadn't heard the last of it. She dared not remain in London, where the press could find her easily enough. She didn't want Kit to be pounced upon and questioned; some journalists were totally without scruple.

During the long trip on the pleasure boat to Greenwich she had thought clearly about her dilemma over Ziggy and realised that she simply could not marry him. It would be a flight from reality for both of them, and it might harm Kit. Christie was deeply disturbed by this new piece of publicity; it put Ziggy into a poor light. Logan would only have to produce that picture to prove that Ziggy was no fit person to be Kit's stepfather. The photo had been blurred, but it had left an indelible impression of dishevelment; both of them had looked like refugees from a wild party, reeling drunkenly away. The picture wouldn't do much for her image, either. It had been a gift to Logan.

The question was—would he use it?

Her parents were very guarded; they carefully

didn't comment on the press stories which she knew they must have read. They welcomed her and Kit with open arms. She spent the following week playing with Kit, helping her mother in the house, enjoying a life style she hadn't had since she left Logan and was plunged into the madhouse of the film world.

Christie made several trips to London to look at houses, leaving Kit with her mother while she drove to the city. She didn't see anything she really liked and began to think she was going to have to settle for a house a little further out. She came back from one of these trips to find her mother in the kitchen preparing the evening meal while her father smoked his pipe in front of the television, watching the news. Christie had been gone all day and was very tired; her feet ached and she was depressed about ever finding anywhere to live.

'Had any luck, darling?' Mrs Mottram asked as Christie walked into the kitchen, and Christie shook her head gloomily.

'I saw several other agents today, but still no luck.' She sniffed the delicious aroma of braising steak. 'That smells good. Is Kit in the garden?'

'No, he's out,' said Mrs Mottram, giving her a guilty look, rather flushed.

'Out?' Christie stiffened. 'Out where? Who with?'

'Don't worry, he's safe. He's with Logan.'

Christie went icy cold from head to foot, staring.

'He arrived just after you left this morning and said he'd like to take Kit out for the day. I didn't know what to do, but Logan is his father, he has a right to see him, and I didn't know where to find you, how to get in touch ... Logan said he was going back to the States tomorrow, it had to be today, and Kit did want to go, Christie, I couldn't refuse.' Mrs Mottram gave her a pleading smile, still uncertain. 'I told Logan to bring Kit back by six, they should be here soon.'

Christie looked at her watch. 'You shouldn't have let Logan take him; where did he say they were going?'

'He said something about the seaside—Kit was thrilled; he misses the sea, you know.'

'Yes.' It was five to six now. Christie looked out of the window. It was still quite sunny, twilight wouldn't be falling for several hours yet. Where had Logan taken Kit? She was nervous and jumpy as she waited, pacing to and fro while her parents watched her anxiously. The clock ticked on past six, past half past six, then it was seven and it was beginning to be dusky; the wind was chill, she listened to it howling around the house, rustling the trees in the forest. Traffic still thundered along the main artery which passed the house on its way to the centre of London; no cars stopped.

'It's very thoughtless of Logan to keep Kit out so long,' Mrs Mottram complained, and Christie turned a pale face to her, her lips bloodless. Fear was possessing her, she didn't dare to put her terror into words.

The phone rang suddenly and they all jumped. Christie ran to answer it, knocking over a chair on the way; she didn't even feel the impact or the bruise which began to form on her calf.

'Hallo?' she whispered.

'Christie?'

'Logan, where the hell are you? Do you know what time it is? How dare you . . .'

'We're in the States,' said Logan, slicing through her words and leaving her dazed and silent.

Her heartbeats slowed until they almost stopped. She couldn't speak, her lips were too dry. She held the phone tightly and knew that it was what she had feared from the minute she knew Logan had appeared and taken Kit away with him. She should have warned her mother; but it hadn't occurred to her. She had thought they were quite safe once they were in England; she had forgotten that Logan still had Kit on his American passport, that he might take the boy back with him to the States, and nobody would question it. Christie had an English passport, of course; and she had had Kit written into that, as her son, but he was Logan's son too and entitled to American citizenship.

'You can't do this, Logan,' she broke out despairingly.

'I've done it,' Logan told her, and his voice was curt. 'Kit is home and he is staying with me from now on. I only rang so that you wouldn't worry about him, he's safe with me. Far safer than he would have been with you and that drunk you're living with.'

The phone clicked and she held it, staring at it dumbly. A great cry came from her throat; she dropped the phone and covered her face with both hands, breaking into tears. Her parents had come out and stood there, horrified, but she wasn't even aware of them, she was lost in a nightmare.

CHAPTER SEVEN

SHE went through the next two days in a daze; deep in shock and hardly believing what was happening. Voices kept breaking through to her and she would turn a pale face to stare at the speaker, her blue eyes darkly ringed with shadow now, her mouth trembling until she bit into it to steady it. The marks of her teeth showed like chilblains in her lip; small sores, darker in colour than the surrounding flesh.

'I can't believe Logan has done such a thing! How could he?' her mother kept saying, sobbing.

'You must be practical,' her father told her. 'First, you must see your lawyer. There are steps which must be taken now, quickly.'

Christie didn't answer either of them; she wasn't speaking, she was thinking about Kit. Logan would look after him, of course; she didn't doubt that, that wasn't what was terrifying her, it was the possibility that she might fail, she might not get Kit back, she might lose him for good. That night she tried to get in touch with her lawyer, but of course he had gone home for the night, and all she got was a recorded message asking callers to ring again after nine next morning. Her mother kept talking to her, trying to break through to her, and now and again she would sob, and Christie would stare at her blankly. She had cried herself out in that first storm of tears, now she was cold and grimly set on fighting to get Kit back.

'You ought to ring the police,' her father told her, and Christie thought: yes, that is what I must do, but when she rang the local people they weren't much help. They were sympathetic, but they gave her the same advice as her father—to see her lawyer. Logan was an American and had taken his son out of English jurisdiction; the original custody order had been made by an American court and it was to American justice that she would have to apply for restitution of her custody rights.

She went to bed but did not sleep; she listened to the forest breathing in the night, the poignant cries of an owl hunting among the trees, the whisper of leaves and the flutter of wings.

Logan would have taken Kit back to Los Angeles. What had he told Kit? Did the child realise that he had been snatched away from his mother? Or did he think he was on holiday and would be coming back to her? She hoped Logan hadn't said anything to Kit which upset him; what frightened her most of all was the fear that Kit might be frightened, that he might be unhappy, that he might be lying awake, too, missing her the way she was missing him.

She counted the hours as they passed without knowing what she was doing; hearing the silvery chime of one of the clocks in the house, waiting for it, watching the sky gradually lighten and the birds begin their morning chorus. She was on tenterhooks as she waited for the day to start; she had to be in London to see her lawyer as soon as his office opened.

'Do you want me to come with you?' Delia Mottram asked her as Christie left the house at eight o'clock, and Christie shook her head.

'I'll be okay, thanks—don't worry, Mum.'

'You didn't eat any breakfast, just black coffee, and you didn't eat last night. You must eat, Christie, you'll be ill if you don't.'

'Let me come with you,' her father pressed, looking anxious. 'You can't go alone, not in this state.'

'I'll be fine,' she said, shaking them off like a dog shedding burrs; she did not want anyone with her, they kept trying to talk to her, kept trying to disturb her intense, deadly concentration on Kit and what she must do to get him back. She didn't have the patience to cope with her parents, their concern and love was another burden for her at that moment. She was aware that they were almost as worried as she was and she loved them for it, she was grateful for their concern, but only one thing mattered to her. She had to find out how she could fight Logan and get back custody of Kit.

She had to wait an hour before she saw the lawyer and he listened in the same bland, calm manner, watching her agitated, bloodless face with thoughtful, appraising eyes. He asked questions, nodded, tapped a pencil on his blotter while he stared at her.

'I am not an expert on American law; off the top of my head I can't give you a definite answer, but at a venture I'd say that your best course, Mrs Gray, would be to return to the States yourself and see your own lawyer over there, preferably the firm which handled the original divorce and

custody settlement. From this side of the Atlantic
it will be time-consuming and difficult to pursue
this matter. If you want to retrieve your son as
soon as possible, you have more chance of doing
that if you yourself are resident in the United
States while making the attempt. You see . . .'

His voice rolled on, sonorous and measured.
Christie listened with a restless impatience.

'Surely there's something I can do? He took Kit
out of this country without my permission!'

'I understand from you that he had visiting
rights? He could see the child whenever he chose?'

'Yes, of course, but he isn't just visiting him,
he's taken Kit back to the States without my
permission!'

'Quite so, but had you consulted him before you
left the United States with the boy?' The lawyer
put the question gently.

Christie stared, lips parted on a soundless gasp,
whitening even more. She couldn't speak, she
merely shook her head.

'I've no doubt at all that his lawyers will make a
strong point of that—how could he visit his son if
he was on the other side of the Atlantic? The
counter-claim will be that it was you who removed
the boy without the father's permission, and I
don't see how you can deny that.'

'On the phone he said he was going to keep Kit,'
she whispered.

'While you live in England there's a strong
possibility that an American court would feel that
the father had a right to custody of his son in
order to bring him up as an American. The boy
has lived there since he was born and is an

American citizen. I'm afraid his father might be able to make out a very strong case for restitution of custody to himself; especially if he produces the evidence which he threatens to show the court— the newspaper photographs and articles which could be seen to prove you no fit person to care for the child.'

'What am I going to do?' Christie muttered despairingly, as much to herself as to the calm man on the other side of the desk. Her heart had sunk as she listened to him. While she waited to see him, she had almost convinced herself that everything was going to be okay; the lawyer would soon take steps to force Logan to give Kit back to her; she had had only a very vague idea of the necessary moves, but she had walked in here full of blind hope and now it had gone.

'Mrs Gray, I could, of course, take up this matter for you and there are certain moves I could make, but in the circumstances of this case I strongly advise you to try to come to some amicable arrangement with the father. On your own admission, he has allowed the boy to live with you for the last five years without interference or contest and has only acted now because you left the United States with your son without advising him of your intentions. An American court has given Mr Gray regular visiting rights which you have deliberately tried to thwart.' He held up a hand as she tried to protest. 'Mrs Gray, that is possibly how it would look to the American court in question, I have no doubt that that is how your husband's lawyer would portray your actions. I suggest . . .'

His voice droned on like a bluebottle in a glass jar and Christie stared at him without seeing him. Halfway through one of his interminable sentences she got up and he stopped talking, staring at her.

'Goodbye,' she said, walking out of the room, and he gazed after her in apparent disbelief that a client should walk out on him while he was at his most brilliant.

Christie drove back to Epping. Her parents were shaken when she told them what the lawyer had told her; her father said: 'Why not see another lawyer? Surely there's something that can be done? Kit could be made a ward of court . . .'

'I'm going back to the States,' Christie said flatly, and went up to pack. Her mother came after her, distraught.

'Darling, what are you going to do? I can't believe that Logan can just walk off with Kit and the law can't force him to give him back—the man you saw in London must be a fool!'

'He was honest, not a fool,' Christie corrected. 'He said there were plenty of things he could do but that they would all take months, maybe even years, and in the end I might not get Kit back, and if I did, Kit might not even remember me. I can't wait for the law to take its course, I've got to get him back now!'

'Do you think Logan will let you see him?'

'I don't know, I'm going to find out.' Christie was packing with frantic urgency and her face was set in angry lines. She had finished crying and feeling helpless, she was beginning to be very angry. 'I don't see why he shouldn't. After all, I let him see Kit, why should he refuse me?'

Mrs Mottram looked at her uncertainly. 'Perhaps when you're back in California, Logan may let you have Kit back anyway?' she suggested with tentative care. 'He may just have resented you taking Kit out of the country without telling him. I thought that was rather thoughtless of you, Christie—after all, Logan is his father, he had a right to know.'

Christie closed her case and locked it, face averted. 'I must ring Janet and tell her,' she said, suddenly remembering. 'She can either fly back with me or follow me.' Janet was American, of course; her family lived in Los Angeles and although she very rarely talked about her private life Christie knew Janet was very fond of her parents and her younger brother, she visited them frequently during her days off work. Janet had had one boy-friend over the past year, but some months ago she had quarrelled with him and since then had not mentioned any man in her life. Janet was not a very communicative girl; she kept herself to herself, Christie wasn't always sure what she was thinking.

When Christie rang and told her the news Janet was upset, taken aback. 'I'm so sorry, Mrs Gray— how worrying for you, but I'm sure Mr Gray will take good care of Kit, he loves him, you know. Try not to worry too much.'

'Will you come back with me or follow me?' Christie asked. 'I'll pay for your ticket home, of course, and for the moment your job is still open—if I get Kit back I'll still need you.'

'When are you leaving?'

'Now, today, the first flight I can get to the West Coast.'

'Where are you?'

'At my family home in Epping. It will take me several hours to get to Heathrow.' Christie was driving a hired car which she would leave at the airport. She was just about to ring and book herself on a flight.

'I'll come with you,' Janet decided slowly. 'I'll meet you at the terminal. What time, do you think?'

'I'll just book the flights then I'll ring and tell you,' Christie said. 'We'll meet near the Pan-Am desk, okay?'

She rang off, rang the airport and booked two seats on a flight that evening. Janet said she would be waiting when Christie arrived; she was already half packed when Christie rang her back. Although Christie had been determined to go alone she felt oddly comforted by the thought of having company on the long exhausting flight, especially as Janet was so quiet and calm. She loved Kit, but she wouldn't cry, the way Delia Mottram was crying now. Christie was deeply attached to her mother, but Delia was highly strung and volatile emotionally; which was why she always had attacks of stage fright before she went on stage, crippling stomach cramp which left her doubled up and white to her hairline. Christie was fighting down her own fear and grief, she didn't want to cope with her mother's. It was so much easier to channel all her feelings into one emotion—anger. It was keeping her active, driving her on as she made all her arrangements to go back to the States; it was giving her the adrenalin she needed to get through the next few days. All that black, harsh anger was going towards Logan; whenever she thought of him she trembled with rage.

'Let us come with you to the airport,' her mother suggested as Gerald Mottram carried Christie's cases downstairs to put them in the boot of her hired car.

'Much better not,' said Christie, kissing her. 'I hate airport farewells.' She followed her father out to the car and Delia came with her, the May wind blowing her hair around her face. She looked haggard today; suddenly much older. Christie wondered if she had the same expression in her own face; she felt as though she did, the skin across her cheekbones was dragged tight, her eyes ached as if she had cried herself blind.

'We'd be happy to come to the States with you,' Gerald Mottram told her, as he slammed the boot down and turned to face her. 'Christie, you may need someone to help you through this . . .'

'I'll manage. I'm not afraid of Logan.' She hugged him. 'But thanks for offering, Dad, it's just like you.'

She turned to hug her mother and Delia said anxiously: 'Oh, Christie, are you sure? You're so pale, I'm worried about you.'

'I'm tougher than I look,' Christie said, remembering the lonely months after she left Logan and had to go through her pregnancy alone in the States. She had been through bad times before and coped with them somehow; even though at times she had been bitterly homesick and longed for her family. She had had to be strong for Kit and she had found reserves of

strength inside herself that she hadn't known
existed. Often it wasn't the big things that
suddenly knocked you down; it was the little
things—a moment at Christmas when you remembered childhood and felt very far from home,
the first crisp morning in autumn which reminded
of the forest rides she had loved as a child, a
birthday parcel in which her mother always
included home-made biscuits, her favourite thin
chocolate shortbreads. At those moments she had
cried and felt homesick and wished briefly that she
was a child again, safe in the white frame house on
the edge of the old forest, but then she had picked
herself up and gone on because she had discovered
when Kit was born that she was an adult, a
woman with a child of her own to love and
protect. She could no longer lean on her parents;
she had Kit leaning on her.

She drove away, watching the small figures of
her parents diminishing in the driving mirror; their
hands pale, fluttering, as they waved. A vague
sadness came over her, she wasn't sure why,
perhaps because it was so long since she had been
a child who believed that they could work
wonders. Growing up imposes a new perspective; a
new understanding, of oneself and everyone
around one. She had grown up long ago; it was
only now, though, that she realised how far she
had come since her wedding day, what a distance
there was between the eighteen-year-old girl who
had defied her parents advice and rushed headlong
into love and marriage—and herself now, grimly
going to battle to get back her child. How
marvellous it would be if she could hand the

problem to someone else, as a child does! Yet
Christie knew she wouldn't do that even if anyone
offered to take the burden from her. Kit was her
child, he had been from birth; her separation from
his father had only made Kit more precious to her,
and she wouldn't give up one hair of his head to
anyone in the world.

As she walked across the airport terminal she
saw Janet waiting, sitting on her suitcase, watching
the passengers flood past. Janet saw her and
waved, smiling. As Christie came up beside her,
Janet touched her arm gently.

'Don't look so worried. We'll soon be in L.A.
and then you'll see Kit. Give me the tickets and I'll
check the cases in—you go and sit down, you look
as if you might faint. You're dead white.'

There was only a few minutes before their flight
was called; Christie sat on one of the seats nearby
and felt unreal. The echoing foyer seemed to swim
around her, the faces of the people walking past
dreamlike. She pulled herself together; she was not
going to faint, she might miss that plane and she
had to get back to Los Angeles.

When they landed at Los Angeles the city was
veiled in yellow smog. Christie knew how little
chance there was of getting a taxi at the airport,
she meant to hire a car, but as they emerged from
Customs they found Ziggy waiting.

'How did you know we were on that flight?'
Christie asked in amazement as he smiled at her.

'I rang your home and they told me.' Ziggy put
an arm around her, his face sombre. 'I'm sorry,
honey, it's my fault, isn't it? Logan wouldn't have
snatched Kit if it hadn't been for me.'

She was too weary to say much; the flight had been so long and tedious, she hadn't slept although she had lain back with closed eyes pretending to sleep because Janet kept watching her and looking worried.

'Don't blame yourself, Ziggy,' she said automatically, but her eyes didn't quite meet his as he walked beside her, watching her. She didn't blame Ziggy, yet she couldn't forget that it had been his loss of control that had triggered Logan into taking Kit away. Ziggy was a delightful friend, a charming companion, but he was weak; when any pressure hit him he took the easiest way out. He had some weird friends, like the bearded rock star at whose party he had got drunk; his life style was one of drift and indifference. She had thought him tolerant and civilised; when in fact Ziggy didn't really care what other people did, he fell in with whatever was going on around him, he accepted what he met without criticism. When he was with Christie she was the image he reflected; when he was with people like Theo Nelson he reflected their morals, their attitudes. Ziggy was a sweet man, but he had no backbone and no personal strength, and perhaps he knew it. Perhaps that explained the curious poignancy of his music; the regret and wistful appeal in it.

'Had you booked into a hotel?' asked Ziggy, putting her into his car while the porter stacked the cases in the boot.

'Not yet; I want to see Kit as soon as possible.' Until she was certain Kit was happy she couldn't think of anything else.

'Your mother thought you hadn't—so I took

the chance of booking you and Janet into the Beverly Hills.'

Christie smiled wryly. 'Thank you, Ziggy, that was very thoughtful of you.' She would never have booked into that hotel; it was far too popular with people from the film world and always crowded. She would have preferred somewhere quiet and anonymous, off the beaten track, but she knew Ziggy had been well-meaning, so she smiled at him without saying what she really thought.

Janet got into the car beside her and a moment later Ziggy drove away slowly, following the tail lights of a car in front because the smog was too thick to drive any faster. 'It's lifting,' said Ziggy with optimism, peering through the windscreen. 'You were lucky to put down in this—flights were cancelled earlier today, the airport was totally fogged in.'

'I think it *is* clearing,' said Janet. 'When we left the airport I could only see one car ahead; now I can see quite a distance.'

They were right. By the time they had reached the hotel, the thick yellow smog had vanished and the day was bright and clear; it was hard to believe that there had ever been any fog. Ziggy had booked Christie a double suite; he came up with her and Janet and insisted on getting them a drink while they sat down. Christie didn't like to ask him to go; he had been so kind and thoughtful and he was obviously feeling guilty. Janet discreetly left them alone and Ziggy came over to sit beside Christie on the couch, taking her hand.

'I feel a heel, Christie—I was selfish, trying to force you to marry me, I should have had more sense. I've caused you a lot of trouble, haven't I? I didn't mean to, you know that, I wish I could help—if there's anything I can do . . .'

'I know, Ziggy, thank you.' Christie smiled up at him, her face set in tired lines. 'I'm sorry, I'm not very bright today. I've got jet-lag and I need a bath and some sleep.'

'Sure,' he said, getting up. 'I'll be on my way, then—you know where I am if you need me. If it would help, I'll talk to your ex-husband, explain that he needn't worry about me any more. He was happy enough to leave Kit with you until I showed up in the picture—if he knows I'm out of it, he'll probably hand Kit back to you.'

'That's very sweet of you, Ziggy, but I have to talk to Logan myself,' Christie explained, and he nodded wryly and left.

She dragged herself into the bathroom and had a long bath; her whole body was limp with exhaustion. She put on a towelling robe, went into her bedroom and sat on the edge of the bed while she rang Logan's home. There was no answer; the phone rang and rang. Christie slowly put the receiver down and lay back on the bed, her arms behind her head. Where was Logan if he wasn't at his own house? Where was Kit? Were they out? Would they be coming back later? Or had Logan taken Kit somewhere else? He might have hidden Kit away somewhere; to stop any legal attempt to remove Kit from his care. She tried to put herself into Logan's situation. What would he do?

She yawned, her eyes closing. She had a

headache, she couldn't think clearly. She hadn't slept or eaten for days now. She felt so light she was floating way above the bed.

Janet tiptoed in and covered her sleeping body with a quilt. Christie didn't stir.

CHAPTER EIGHT

CHRISTIE slept for six hours and woke up in the dark, disorientated for a moment, unable to remember where she was, then she remembered and stumbled off the bed, put on the light and dialled Logan's number again. There was a short pause, then the ringing stopped and she heard his voice.

'Hallo?'

Christie put down the phone. He was at home, which meant Kit must be there. She went into the bathroom and showered, dressed in jeans and a thin blue shirt, then had a short talk with Janet.

'I'm moving out of here tomorrow,' she told her. 'I'm going to hire a car and stay at a quiet motel I know near Logan's house. Why don't you go on home for a few days, Janet, stay with your family? I'll be in touch when I know my plans. I promise I'll let you know as soon as I can whether I'll be needing you or not. It all depends . . .' her voice trailed away, she couldn't put it into words.

'I know,' Janet said lightly. 'I'll wait to hear from you. I already got myself a car, by the way; I knew we were going to need one in L.A. You can use mine if you want to drive over to see Kit tonight.'

'Oh, thank you, Janet, you're a dear,' said Christie, smiling impulsively at her. 'If Ziggy rings . . .'

'I saw him. I went down to the pool earlier and he came in—I told him you were sleeping, and couldn't be disturbed. I don't think he believed me, but he's too sweet a guy to show it. He sent his love.'

Christie sighed. 'Poor Ziggy!'

Janet gave her a dry look. 'He'll do okay, don't worry about him. When I left the pool he was sitting chatting up a cute redhead in a skimpy bikini, and he didn't look like a guy on the point of falling apart.'

Christie broke out laughing; Janet's down-to-earth comment had punctured her mood, deflated her. Janet was right; Ziggy would be okay. What made her think she was that important to him? Men have died, but not for love, Janet's amused eyes said, and that was so right. Love may give a man a headache, even a heartache, but it doesn't kill him. Kit needed her, he was a child, he couldn't stand alone. Ziggy was a grown man and could take care of himself.

'He'll get over you,' said Janet.

'Of course he will.' Christie looked at her watch. 'I'm hungry, it seems hours since I ate. Let's have something sent up, then I'm going out for a drive.'

'Alone?' Janet frowned, looking at her uneasily.

'I'm going over to see my ex-husband,' Christie explained. 'I think I'd better wait until Kit's asleep. I wouldn't want him to see me beating his father's head in!'

'No,' agreed Janet, smiling. 'That wouldn't do much for his sense of security.' She picked up the phone and dialled Room Service. 'What would you like?'

Christie had a chef's salad of diced chicken, ham and walnuts bound in a light, lemony mayonnaise on a bed of crisp mixed salad, followed by fruit and coffee. While she slept her mind seemed to have cleared; she felt calm and sure of herself now. She had recovered her appetite along with her self-confidence; the desperation and urgency had gone. She felt she could face Logan without losing control, without breaking up in tears. For a short time, after she realised he had taken Kit away from her, she had regressed to near adolescence, trembling with panic, her anger and her grief in charge of her. She hadn't eaten, hadn't slept, she had burnt up energy at a terrific rate and hadn't replaced it, and she was relieved that she hadn't confronted Logan in that state of mind because he would have had a walk-over with her. She was going to need all her wits and self-control, if she was to persuade Logan to let Kit go back to her, without a long, unpleasant legal battle. She would face that if she had to, too, but she hoped she could talk Logan into realising how painful that would be for their son. If Kit wasn't to grow up caught between the crossfire of their enmity they had to come to terms. The one person who mattered in all this was Kit.

'Where's this car, then?' she asked Janet as she slipped on a cashmere sweater she had bought in London and neatly folded the cuffs of her blue shirt back over the cuffs of the sweater. She looked cool and trim, almost workmanlike, except that the cashmere had a very elegant air and her face and hair were far too feminine to belong to a boy.

'Here are the keys. Sure you don't want me to

come with you? I could wait in the car,' Janet suggested, and Christie shook her head.

'Thanks, but I'll go alone.' This was one interview she would prefer to face without witnesses.

Janet came down with her in the lift and showed her the car. She stood watching Christie drive away, and Christie hoped she didn't look as worried as Janet did; she didn't feel worried any more, she had an almost fatalistic calm. Oddly, the worst had happened. She had lost Kit. She had been on the floor, defeated, desperate, but now she was climbing back up off her knees full of the adrenalin of determination. Somehow she was going to persuade Logan to give Kit back. She knew it. The anger still burned inside her somewhere, she was furious with Logan, but for Kit's sake she wasn't going to let herself rip, she wasn't going to lose her temper or her head.

Logan lived in a quiet avenue on the Pasadena side of Los Angeles. His house was colonial, white-walled with a terracotta roof and a pillared terrace running along the back of it, set among smooth lawns. Along the driveway flowered some cherry trees whose white blossom floated off on a night breeze. There wasn't a sound in the residential street, nobody was around, but most of the houses showed lighted windows and she heard televisions babbling in some of them.

Christie parked and got out of the car. Logan's ironwork gates creaked as she pushed them open and she looked quickly at the house. There was no light at the front of it, but she knew that Logan usually sat in a spacious room at the back, leading on to the terrace. That was where he had all his stereo equipment and the records and tapes, where he listened to music or watched TV or read.

As she walked softly up the drive her nostrils picked up the scent of flowers in the garden and the damp evening smell of grass. Logan had bought this place during the last year of their marriage, she hadn't liked it half as much as the apartment they had had for a few months right in Los Angeles, near the bay. That had been noisy and slightly shabby, but it had been homely, cosy, she had felt she fitted. She hadn't felt that this elegant, expensive house was a place for her. Logan had said it would make a wonderful family home, and that word had made her want to run, of course. She hadn't been ready to settle down to playing happy families, not for years.

Just as Christie reached the house the door opened. She froze in the shadows, thinking Logan had seen her, but then saw that a woman stood in the brick porch.

Christie ducked out of sight behind a massive flowering bush growing up the side of the house. She heard the woman laughing as she came out on to the drive.

'You're crazy, Logan!' Christie shrank into the shadows, peering through close-set leaves. They were walking past her and talking, they didn't look in her direction. Christie could see them both clearly. The woman was slim and graceful, with black hair wound into a chignon high on the back of her head. Her aquamarine dress clung to her body; it was silk, and she shivered slightly as a little wind blew through it. Logan put an arm round her.

'Cold? Here, borrow my sweater, you can give it back to me tomorrow.' He pulled a black sweater over his head and smiled down at the other woman and Christie felt a bitter, angry jealousy. It was stupid, senseless—she told herself so, but it didn't make the emotion go away. Logan was a free agent, of course he must have had other women, why shouldn't he? He was a very attractive man, and he wasn't Christie's property, and her reason told her that it was absurd to watch him with someone else and resent it.

'It suits you, Bel,' said Logan, laughing, as the dark-haired woman deftly wriggled herself into the thin sweater.

'Does it?' Laughing, the woman looked down. It certainly outlined her curves, Christie thought sourly, disliking her. She had a smooth, calm face which came close to real beauty. Christie did not like her.

'Better than it does me,' Logan grinned, and he was right. On the woman the sweater was sexy. 'Thanks for coming tonight,' he went on, and the woman put a finger on his mouth, shaking her head.

'Don't thank me—I had a wonderful time, it was terrific, I loved every minute of it.'

They began to walk down the driveway to the gate. 'You're sure?' queried Logan. 'You'll be able to make it again tomorrow?'

'Wild horses wouldn't keep me away,' the woman said, her voice coming faintly to Christie as they moved further away. Christie watched, rigid with resentment, and when they halted at the gate with their backs towards the house she slid along the wall and ducked into the porch. She stood in the hallway, listening, but there wasn't a sound in the house. Through a door on the left she saw a lighted room; that was the long sitting-room which Logan used and no doubt they had been in there, listening to music together. After making love? she wondered, as she saw cushions scattered on the carpet. While her son slept innocently upstairs had Logan and his lady-friend been making it on the floor in there?

Her face burned, she turned and ran up the stairs, and began opening doors. She found Kit on the third try. She heard his breathing as she stood in the doorway. He was fast asleep; a small hump in the bed, the sheet up to his ears and only his dark hair visible. Christie felt tears sting her eyes. She went softly over to the bed and touched his hair, very lightly, so as not to wake him.

It would be easy to wake him, dress him and take him away while Logan was busy saying goodbye to his woman at the gate. She was tempted, but it might worry and alarm Kit. Heaven alone knew what psychological damage might be done by a furtive escape from his father's house in the middle of the night. And what if Logan caught them? There would be a nasty scene; and Christie didn't want to inflict that on Kit.

She watched his rosy, unconscious face tenderly. He looked happy, anyway. She bent and kissed his hair and then turned away to tiptoe out of the room. As she came out of the door, Logan emerged from a room farther along the landing, a white sweater in his hand, his bronzed chest bare.

They both froze, staring at each other. Logan's

grey eyes were hard, she saw him thinking fast, his glance moved past her into Kit's room, his brows jerking together, then he took two long strides and stared past her into the shadowy bedroom, checking that Kit was there and the room was empty except for him.

Christie began to run towards the top of the stairs. Logan closed Kit's door quietly and came after her, running in silence on the thick carpet. By the time Christie had reached the foot of the stairs she was calming down, her panic over. She had come to see Logan, why was she running away from him? She was about to halt and turn to face him when he caught up with her; his fingers biting into her upper arm.

'Oh, no, you don't!' he snapped, jerking her round to face him, and, off balance, she put out her hands to stop herself falling as her feet slid from under her, on the polished tiled floor. That was a mistake. She touched Logan's bare chest and gasped in shock, snatching her hands away, trembling.

Logan's eyes narrowed to glittering points of light at the betraying response; her face filled with hot colour and she looked down, swallowing. Logan let go of her and there was a strange, charged silence.

Then he said: 'How did you get in here? When did you take up burglary?'

She shrugged, still not looking at him because she was afraid of what her eyes might tell her. 'The door was open; I just walked in.'

His voice was thoughtful. 'While I was taking Bel to her car, I suppose.'

Christie's eyes lifted then, her hands shaking with the desire to hit him. 'Yes, while you were kissing your lady-friend goodnight,' she said contemptuously. 'You had a nerve, criticising me over Ziggy—but then, I suppose, it's okay for you to have your women here with Kit upstairs asleep! One law for men, another for women; that's what you think, isn't it?'

He stared at her oddly without answering, then glanced up the stairs and said in a low voice: 'Are you trying to wake him up? Come in here if you're going to scream the house down,' and propelled her with a hand in the small of her back into the lighted room she had glanced at earlier. Christie picked her way scornfully over the scattered cushions.

'You *do* seem to have had fun,' she said with iced distaste.

Logan closed the door and leaned against it. Christie looked round at him and away again. 'Do you mind putting on that sweater?' she asked pointedly.

He tossed it on to a chair. 'Is it bothering you?' he taunted, moving towards her, the light gleaming on his tanned skin. Christie turned her head away, she didn't want to see those broad, powerful shoulders and the black wedge of hair curling up from his midriff, roughening the centre of his bronzed chest, she didn't want to feel the magnetic drag of the senses which it might cause inside her. She had come here to try to persuade him to give Kit up; she didn't want her mind clouded by desire, especially knowing that he had been in here earlier with that other woman. She hated herself because of the instinctive jealousy she had felt; it was humiliating to admit it even in the privacy of her own head.

She sat down on the white couch behind her and Logan stood in front of her, his legs apart and his hands on his hips in a casual stance which didn't lessen her feeling of threat.

'What are you doing here in the middle of the night?' he asked softly, and without waiting for an answer went on: 'Let me guess . . . you came to snatch Kit back. If I hadn't caught you, you'd be sneaking out of the house with him now. Is your boy-friend waiting outside in a car?' He watched her angry face. 'No? So you decided to do it on your own.'

'I wasn't intending to kidnap him back,' Christie retorted fiercely. 'Do you really think I'd sneak in here and drag him out of bed when he was fast asleep, make him get dressed and creep out of the house, risking being caught and having a blazing row with you while Kit listened?' She looked at him bitterly. 'You may not care whether you upset him or not, but I do!'

'Then what were you doing up there?'

'I wanted to see him, that's all. I was careful not to wake him up, but I had to know he was all right.' Her voice shook slightly and her eyes glistened. Logan looked at her and then turned and walked over to a cabinet on the other side of the room. He opened it and produced a bottle of brandy, poured two glasses and came back to her. He put one into her hand.

'Drink it.'

'I don't want . . .'

'You need it. Drink it.' Christie resented the whiplash tone, but she felt too close to tears to clash with him again; she lifted the brandy glass to her mouth and swallowed some of the liquid, shuddering as the heat reached her throat.

'How could you take him away like that?' she broke out suddenly. 'Don't you know what that did to me? It was a nightmare, having Kit vanish, wondering if he was frightened or . . .'

'Why should he be frightened with me?' Logan interrupted harshly. 'Why should you be worried *knowing* he was with me? I'm his father—have you forgotten that?'

'You had no right to do it!'

'I had every right—once I discovered that not only did you plan to marry that drunk you've been playing around with, but that you meant to stay in England! You were the one who took Kit away. You meant to stop me seeing him.'

'No!'

'Oh, yes, Christie! When I was on one side of the world and Kit was on the other, how was I supposed to see him more than once or twice a year? What sort of father–son relationship could we have had? We'd be strangers, and I wasn't going to let that happen. If I snatched Kit, it was because you pushed me into it.'

Christie burned with anger, but she caught back the words she wanted to yell at him. She looked down, fighting for self-control. She had to come to terms with Logan or she would never get Kit back without a long-drawn-out legal fight which would scar all of them.

After a silence she asked: 'Does Kit know?'

'That I snatched him? No, do you take me for a fool?'

She looked up and her bitter eyes spoke for her. Logan's mouth twisted. 'As far as Kit's aware, he's having a holiday with me,' he said drily. 'You're not the only one who doesn't want him upset.'

She gave a brief sigh of relief. 'At least that's something,' she muttered, and finished her brandy. Logan swallowed the rest of his and took her glass, placing both glasses on a small side-table. Christie looked around the room; it had been redecorated since she last saw it. The walls were lined with bookshelves crammed with books and set into them was Logan's massive stereo music-deck, all chrome and glass, beneath it a row of cupboards which she knew hid his collection of records and tapes. The curtains were new; floor-length deep blue glazed cotton, but the carpet was the same, she remembered the creamy ivory of the background and the green and red and blue of the geometric pattern in the centre.

Logan was picking up the scattered cushions and flinging them into chairs and on to the couch beside Christie. She watched him coldly.

'Who is she?'

He looked at her through his dark lashes, smiling as though she was amusing him, and Christie did not like that expression, it infuriated her. 'Bel?' he drawled. 'She's a friend of mine.'

'So I noticed—the sort of friend you play very private games with,' she snapped, and he laughed softly.

'Why are you so acid about her? You wouldn't be jealous, would you?'

She went scarlet, fizzing with rage. 'No, I wouldn't! Don't kid yourself.'

'It isn't me who's kidding myself,' Logan said drily. 'You've been spitting like a wildcat every time you mentioned her.'

'I don't like double standards. You want me to live like a nun because you claim it might harm Kit for me to have a man around, but you had her here—and don't tell me she came to discuss literature with you, because I wouldn't believe you.'

'I wasn't going to claim anything of the kind,' said Logan, and sat down beside her. Christie stiffened, looking at him with acute wariness. She didn't want him so close.

'Where were you hiding in the garden?' he asked casually, as though merely curious.

'Behind a bush,' she said with defiance, and he laughed.

'You're lucky nobody spotted you and called the police. In this district people suspect every shadow. We've had a lot of break-ins over the past year. You would have looked pretty silly being dragged off to jail, the press would have had a field day.' He grinned sideways at her, his eyes mocking. 'And I wouldn't have gone bail for you, either.'

'I just bet you wouldn't,' she muttered.

'So why are you here?' he asked, smiling.

'Why do you think? You didn't think I'd leave Kit with you, did you? I want him back. If I have to, I'll apply to the courts to have my custody restored, but I don't have to tell you what a long-drawn-out legal wrangle would do to Kit, do I? He was only a baby when custody was settled in the beginning, but he's old enough now to understand what's going on.'

'That's why I'm not prepared to leave him in your hands,' Logan said brusquely. 'I want some say in how my son grows up. The guy you're living with is a drunk with some very odd friends, and that's not the sort of influence I want for Kit.'

'I'm not living with Ziggy!'

'You plan to marry him, don't lie to me!'

'No!' she said angrily, looking at him directly. 'I am not going to marry Ziggy, not now, not ever. Does that satisfy you?'

'Not necessarily,' he said, coolly, watching her with fixed, intent eyes. 'You might simply live with him. I don't suppose it would bother him whether it was legal or not. I'd hardly have described him as ultra-moral or conventional.'

Christie was shaking with rage, her hands clenched. 'I'm not going to live with him either! I doubt if I'll see much of him after this. I admit, I might have married him, we had discussed it—but you've made that impossible.' She gave him a bitter smile. 'I hope that makes you feel pleased with yourself.'

He didn't answer, he just watched her impassively, and Christie bit her lip. 'Don't make me fight you in the courts to get Kit back, Logan. Please . . .'

'Were you in love with Molyneaux?' was all he asked, without answering her question.

Christie dumbly shook her head, and he smiled, wryly.

'No, I didn't think you were. You just drifted

into that relationship blindly, without any idea about the sort of man you were dating, and you'd probably have married him just as blindly. You may be shrewd and clever where your career is concerned, but what you know about men could be written on a postage stamp.'

'I know all I want to about *you*!' Christie snapped, bristling.

'Do you now?' Logan said softly, and she felt a prickle of nervous agitation under his assessing stare. He smiled with crooked mockery as her eyes shifted away. 'What's the matter, Christie? You look like a girl in the last stages of panic.' He moved closer and she shrank back, her breathing too fast and her heartbeat going into overdrive. 'Don't back off,' he said, in that lazy mockery, and his hand caught her chin and turned her face towards him. 'If you know so much about me, tell me what I'm thinking now.'

Their eyes met and she knew precisely what he was thinking, her whole body pulsed with her awareness. She was afraid. It hadn't worked in the past, she didn't want to risk another try. There was still that sexual magnetism between them, she couldn't deny that, but other things hadn't changed, either. She still wanted a career and Logan was still the same man who had tried to force her to choose him instead of her work.

She forced a smile. 'I came to ask you if I could see Kit. Will you let me take him out for the day tomorrow?'

Logan's hand dropped, his face changed. 'Alone? Not on your life,' he said tersely.

'That's not fair—I have a right to see him! You can't refuse me.'

'If you want to see Kit, you'll see him here when I'm around to make sure you don't try to make off with him.'

'The way *you* did!' she snapped, and Logan nodded coolly.

'Exactly. You can visit Kit tomorrow afternoon at two o'clock. Stay as long as you like, I'll take the time off work.'

Christie got up. 'Who's looking after Kit when you aren't here?'

Logan smiled, 'Bel.'

Christie stared at him, bristling. 'Oh, is she?'

Logan looked amused. Blandly he said: 'Bel's wonderful with children.'

'How versatile! I suppose she cooks like a dream, too?'

'Pastry light as air,' he agreed.

'All the feminine virtues, in fact—how nice for you,' Christie said with vicious sweetness, and he laughed.

'Sure you won't stay tonight?' His eyes provoked her and she felt her ears buzz with the beating of her blood. She turned and walked out and she was running away, and Logan knew it. She was afraid of what might happen if the volatile chemical mix between them exploded into a sexual blaze she couldn't put out.

'I'll come back tomorrow at two, then,' she said in the porch.

'I'll be here,' Logan promised with an emphasis she registered with alarm. As she drove back to her hotel through the thick Los Angeles traffic making for Sunset Boulevard she was intensely conscious of her body; the blood beating in her veins, the air drawn into and expelled from her lungs, her skin, bone, muscle and the living filaments of hair, all that made up the woman that she was. Logan had that effect on her; he made her more vitally aware of herself and of him. They were opposed, separate, apart—convex and concave, dark and light, night and day—all the elements which exist of themselves and yet must merge to become a whole.

It could be so simple; yet it was inextricably complicated by the minds that inhabited those bodies. She remembered all too vividly how their bodies fitted together—and how far apart their minds had been. Sexually yoked in harmony, in bed; but out of it pulling in opposite directions like two plunging horses.

Christie was afraid. She was going to have to see Logan, if she wanted to see their son, but she would have given anything at that moment to be a million miles away.

CHAPTER NINE

JANET left very early next day to spend a week with her married sister in Palm Springs, and Christie spent the morning shopping along Rodeo Drive in the high fashion shops where the very rich of Beverly Hills congregated. She met several people she knew very well and smiled at even more whom she hardly knew at all. In one of the larger department stores she ran into Ziggy, who had just bought an oxblood leather jacket which he insisted on showing her. 'Real ox, darling,' he said, and she gave him a helpless smile.

'Idiot!'

'Well, it must be real something—you should have seen the price! Come and have a drink.'

'At this hour?'

'Coffee, then?' he pleaded, looking comic and pathetic all at once, and she gave in, laughing, and rode up in the lift with him to the coffee house on the fourth floor of the store. It was crowded with people and Christie and Ziggy got stared at, but luckily there were far more famous people circulating around the store that day. They got a table in a corner and sat down to drink their coffee without being interrupted.

'Still going to chuck films for the stage?' asked Ziggy after she had told him she was seeing Kit that afternoon, and she nodded, her chin up. Christie was determined on that, anyway.

'What will you do if your ex-husband fights you for custody?'

'Fight back.'

'But what if he won't let you take Kit out of the States again? You won't be able to get a job in London, then.'

'There are theatres elsewhere—come to that, there are theatres right here in L.A. I wanted to work in London because it's my home and it also happens to have some of the best theatre in the world, but it isn't the only place that has good theatre. I'll find stage work somewhere *and* keep Kit.'

Ziggy's wry gaze registered her new calm and self-confidence. He smiled, nodding. 'I just bet you will!'

Two women passed their table, staring, whispering. Christie ignored them and caught the eye of another actor at a table nearby; he winked at her and she smiled back. Ziggy looked round and grinned at him too. They had all worked together on a film a couple of years ago, but Christie hadn't seen the actor since; he had flown off to Italy to make a film and she had stayed in California. For a few weeks they had been good friends; talking, playing cards in a caravan on location for hours, eating meals together, swapping life histories. And then they had said goodbye and now she couldn't remember his surname, only that he was a guy called Bill, and lived in the same unreal world as herself.

She looked at her watch. 'I have to go soon, Ziggy.'

'So do I,' he said. 'I'm shopping—I'm off to

New York tomorrow to start work on the score for this new film; the writer lives there and he wants to write some of the lyrics, God help us. I don't know what zombie said okay to that, but I wish I had my hands round his throat. I once worked with a genius, the best producer I ever met, he had three unbreakable rules and the first one was: keep the writers off the set.'

They parted outside the department store and Christie drove herself back to her hotel to have lunch and collect her cases. She had hired a car early that morning; she meant to check in at a motel before going on to see Kit, but while she was eating in the restaurant she ran into some more old friends and couldn't get away from them. It was just after two when she pulled up outside Logan's house. As she got out of the car Kit came tearing down the drive. He flung himself into her arms and she kissed him, picking him up. Logan had followed him. Christie glanced at him over Kit's head; their eyes met in wary appraisal and her pulses began hammering. Every time she saw him she got the same immediate sensual shock. I won't let it happen again, she thought, almost with despair. Why does he do this to me? Why him, out of all the men in the world? It would all be so much simpler, so much more convenient, if she had fallen for Ziggy or someone else in her own world, someone whose life style merged with her own and who understood her ambition and her need to act.

Kit was peering over her shoulder into the car. 'Oh, you've brought your cases, you're staying with me and Daddy,' he said breathlessly. 'Daddy,

Mummy's staying! We're all going to live here.' He
flung his arms tightly round her neck, almost
strangling her, and Christie gave Logan a look of
alarm and distress. He smiled drily at her and said
nothing; leaving it to her to disillusion Kit.
Christie seethed, wondered how to break it to her
son that she didn't intend to stay in the same
house. With Logan? she thought, her stomach
sinking. Never, and the clamour of her blood at
the very idea made her go bright pink.

'Kit, you see . . .' she began falteringly, and Kit
loosened his grip to look up at her expectantly,
eyes so bright she wanted to cry. 'Well, you're
having a little holiday with Daddy and . . .'

'And you're coming too,' he prompted as she
stopped again. 'I'll bring one of the cases, Daddy,
let me carry one.' He wriggled to get down and
Christie lowered him, her eyes on Logan, silently
begging him to intervene. Logan went on smiling,
his hands on his hips and a wicked amusement in
his eyes. Kit struggled to pull the smallest case out
of the car. Christie bent to take it from him, 'No,
Kit, you don't understand,' she began again.

'I can carry it, Mummy. I can!' He pushed her
hand away and with a terrific jerk pulled the case
out. It landed on Christie's foot and she yelped.
Logan lifted the case off and Kit set off with it
into the house, his small body visibly wrestling
with the weight. Christie massaged her foot,
glaring at Logan.

'You might have said something helpful,' she
muttered in a low voice.

He pulled another case out of the car. 'Why
should I?'

'I can't stay here, you know that!'

'There's plenty of room.' He walked away carrying a case in each hand and a small travelling case under one arm. Christie pursued him, quivering with temper.

'You really think I'd spend a night under the same roof as you? I've no intention of doing anything of the kind!'

He halted and looked down at her, his face hard. 'Tell Kit that. You saw how excited he was—for the first time in his life he thinks he's going to have a mother and father at the same time. Just now he looked as if it was Christmas and the Fourth of July all rolled into one. If you want to tell him he made a mistake, go ahead. Tell him. But don't ask me to help you because I won't stamp on his dreams.' He walked away with her cases and Christie stared after him, biting her lip and feeling one inch high.

It was a fine, clear morning; the air warm as it fanned her face and the sky an impossible, Technicolor blue, the garden was full of heady scents and the birds were in an agitated mood as they flew back and forth to feed the fledglings in their nests. Christie walked slowly up the driveway. Kit had already disappeared into the cool interior of the house. Logan followed him under the porch and Christie heard them both upstairs as she stood in the hall, wondering what she was going to do; she dreaded seeing Kit's face when she told him she wasn't staying, but she certainly didn't want to sleep in this house, with Logan only a room away.

Kit came running down and jumped into her

arms again, hugging her. 'You're going to have the room next to me. Is Janet coming too?'

'No, she's going to stay with her sister in Palm Springs for a week.' Christie brushed the dark hair off his forehead. 'Have you had a good time staying with Daddy?'

'Yes, we went to the races at Los Alamitos and I won some money, my horse was black and he was called Blue Lightning. I bought a lorry with my winnings; it tips up and I can put sand in it.'

'That's nice,' Christie smiled.

'And we went fishing at San Pedro. I didn't catch anything, but I helped Daddy pull in this great big fish—it was that long!' Kit spread his arms as far as they could go and Christie looked derisively at Logan as he joined them.

'*Isn't* your daddy clever?' she cooed.

Logan's grey eyes promised reprisals for the mockery Kit did not hear, nodding excitely in agreement, then Kit said: 'I want to get down. Come and see my lorry, it's on the terrace, Daddy doesn't want sand all over the house.'

She followed him across the spacious sitting-room on to the open terrace. There was a covered sandpit at one end of it; Kit ran there and flung himself down on to his knees beside the large yellow toy lorry. Christie knelt beside him, aware of Logan watching her. She heard the creak of wicker as Logan sat down in a woven chair with a large fan-shaped back. Kit was trundling his sand-laden lorry towards the pit; he tipped the contents out and began refilling the lorry again immediately.

Christie watched and played with him for half

an hour until he tired of the game and suggested that they should play on the lawn. He produced a baseball bat and a catcher's mitt. 'Daddy, come and play too!' he invited confidently. 'Daddy's teaching me to catch,' he told Christie, who nodded while her eyes slid sideways at Logan.

'*Do* you play baseball?' Logan enquired drily, knowing very well that she hadn't a clue about the game.

'I can learn,' she said, gritting her teeth at the teasing. It was a warm day by Beverly Hills standards; a very hot day by English standards. An hour later Christie's thin shirt was sticking to her and she felt perspiration trickling down between her breasts. Her legs ached with running to and fro after the ball which Kit was only too happy to hit when he could and which Logan sent right the way across the large garden. As she panted back with the ball, her face heated, her body drooping, Logan studied her thoughtfully.

'I think we'd better stop now before your mummy flakes out,' he told Kit, who protested,

'Oh, not yet, Mummy, we're having fun—don't you *love* baseball?' It wasn't a question, it was a passionate statement, and Christie bared her teeth at Logan when he laughed.

'It's fun,' she agreed, swallowing. 'But I think I'll take a shower now, I'm so hot I'm melting.'

Kit thought that was funny, he chuckled helplessly and tumbled on to the grass to roll about, kicking his legs. Christie walked back into the house and Logan followed, leaving Kit on the lawn.

'The bathroom is the first door on the right after

Kit's room,' he told her, then he added softly: 'Need any help?'

Christie checked that Kit was out of earshot and then turned on him, trembling with rage. 'You can stop that right here! Save it for your girl-friend. If you're seeing her tonight, I'd be glad if you'd take her elsewhere. I don't want her around while I'm here.'

'I won't need her while you're here,' he said lazily, and her face burned at what she thought were the implications behind the remark. She looked at him with hatred.

'Oh, no—if you think I'm taking her place, you're wrong.' She felt a bitter taste in her throat at the very idea of allowing Logan to substitute her for his usual bedmate. 'You sicken me!' she burst out, her hands clenched. 'Do you really think I'd let you ... I'd rather die! I'm sorry for her; if she heard what you just said she'd ...'

'Perfectly understand,' Logan interrupted, and she looked at him incredulously.

'You can't believe that! You can't be serious? If it was true, what sort of woman can she be?'

'The sort whose two children are at boarding school and who misses them so much she's happy to come and babysit for me when I have to go out and leave Kit,' Logan said drily.

Christie stared, eyes wide and dazed, too shaken to say anything.

Logan studied her. 'Bel's husband works for me. They're good friends of mine. I rang Bel earlier and told her I wouldn't need her to babysit tonight as you were here.' He smiled. 'Last night she came over to cook dinner because she and Bob were spending the evening here. Bob drove off to get some oil in their car; it was overheating and he was worried about it. He was waiting for Bel out on the road; didn't you see a big guy in a check shirt sitting in an estate car?'

Christie shook her head slowly. 'I didn't notice anyone.' She had been too busy thinking about Kit, worrying about Logan's reaction when she appeared. She looked up at Logan, fizzing with temper. 'But you let me think that she . . . why didn't you tell me all this last night?'

'Why should I? You were having quite a time convincing yourself that I was making it with her. I just let you get on with it.'

Christie turned and stamped up the stairs. He had enjoyed watching her lose her temper over the other woman; no doubt it had given his ego a boost. She could kick herself now for letting him see the jealousy she had hated to feel; it was her own fault, he was right, she should have hidden her reactions but last night she hadn't been able to control those instinctive stabs of jealousy.

She found her room, her cases piled on the pink carpet beside the silk-spread bed under a small four-poster whose curtains matched the pale cream curtains hanging at the windows, and when she had unpacked to find a towelling robe, went into the bathroom and showered. Her skin was covered in perspiration; naked under the stinging needles of clear water, she stood with closed eyes letting her body cool, but it did not slow the over-rapid action of her pulse, she still felt hectic, over-wrought. She must be crazy to let herself be stampeded into staying here, under the same roof as Logan. She knew what she was inviting; his grey eyes were far too easy to read, she was asking for trouble if she stayed.

She stepped out of the glass cubicle and slipped into her robe, tying it tightly around her waist. Her hair was dark with water, it clung damply to her scalp and neck. She brushed it, staring at herself in the long wall mirror.

Her eyes were unfamiliar, she didn't recognise them with those over-large pupils, glistening black with excitement, darkening the whole colour of the blue iris. Her mouth was unsteady, her cheeks still flushed, she was trembling. Staring at herself, she fought to get control. She ought to leave now, before it was too late. Logan had manoeuvred her into this; it would be insane to let him win simply because she couldn't summon up the courage to defeat him. Her reason and her senses were fighting and her reason was losing.

She went into her bedroom and bolted the door. When she had dressed in jeans and a clean white shirt she unpacked the rest of her clothes and hung them in the fitted wardrobes taking up one side of the room. All the time while she worked her mind was arguing: 'Get out, get out while you can,' but she was moving like an automaton, she didn't act on those agitated warnings.

She went downstairs and Kit ran to meet her, clasping his arms around her slim waist. 'Are you going to make my tea? I'm hungry. Can I have banana sandwiches and ice-cream?'

Logan walked past, grinning. 'I'm going to have a shower now, it's your turn,' he said. 'His taste-buds are out of key; his favourite food seems to be peanut butter or hamburgers. I don't think you're bringing him up properly.'

Christie ignored that and shepherded Kit into the enormous kitchen. He climbed on to a stool in the dining area at the end by the window and Christie made him some tiny sandwiches and poured him some milk. When he had eaten she took him back into the sitting-room to watch a cartoon show on the television. Logan put his head round the door at a quarter to six.

'I have to go out for a few hours. Will you put Kit to bed? There's plenty of food in the freezer, help yourself.'

Kit ran over to kiss him goodnight. Christie watched, wondering where Logan was going. He was wearing an elegant blue suit and a striped blue shirt; she didn't believe he was keeping a business appointment. He was dressed for a date. Had he lied about the black-haired woman she had seen here last night? Was he meeting her somewhere?

As he straightened from hugging Kit, he gave her a brief glance. 'Don't wait up for me,' he said mockingly, the tanned skin taut over his cheekbones, and Christie stiffened with resentment.

'I wasn't intending to,' she snapped, and was sure that he was meeting a woman. Why else would he be staying out late, dressed to kill?

When he had gone, she put Kit to bed and sat beside him for a while, telling him a bedtime story before he fell asleep. The house was quiet, but her imagination was very active; she felt restless and frustrated, prowling around the house listening to the silence pressing down on her head, the soft warm whisper of the night breeze through the acacias in the garden. She felt a fool. She had been fighting her own compulsive attraction to Logan, dreading the moment when Kit went to bed and they were dangerously alone in the house, and after all Logan had gone off to meet someone else! How stupid could you get?

She went to bed early and bolted her door in defiance, although she didn't expect Logan to try it, not any more. Obviously his attention was elsewhere; he might have been flirting with her, taunting her, but he hadn't any serious intentions and she had let her hectic imagination run away with her. She lay in the darkness, trying to sleep but listening all the time for the sound of his return. It was nearly eleven, she saw by her bedside clock. She turned over. She had to get to sleep. She must stop thinking about Logan. They had been divorced for four years and she hadn't spent her time worrying about where he was or who he was with—why was she doing it now? She tried to think about work, about Kit, about Ziggy, but sleep didn't come.

The last time she looked at her clock it was gone midnight, and Logan still wasn't back yet. She must have fallen asleep soon after that. When she woke up it was daylight and Kit was tapping on her door, calling her.

'Mummy, Mummy, can we have breakfast?'

Christie yawned, sliding out of the bed. 'I won't be a minute, Kit,' she called, and drew the curtains to let the golden light flood into the room; she looked at it bitterly, it was always so sunny here—why couldn't it rain just once in a while? She felt stupidly depressed, she didn't know why. Over

breakfast Kit was lively and talkative and Christie
tried to be as cheerful. Logan must still be asleep,
no doubt he needed the rest. Maybe he wasn't
going to work today.

He appeared five minutes later in a light grey
suit and a shirt in a darker shade. Christie looked
at him resentfully. She was just loading the
dishwasher and she didn't intend to start making
breakfast for him. He should have had it with his
lady-friend.

'I'm late,' he said briskly. 'I'll grab a cup of
coffee and run.'

'The coffee's cold,' said Christie with a grim
satisfaction, and he shrugged, walking out again.

'I'll get some coffee at the office.'

She heard his car drive off and slammed the
front of the dishwasher so hard the glasses in it
rattled and tinkled. Kit looked round, mouth
open.

'You broke a glass,' he said accusingly.

'Oh, dear,' she said unrepentantly. 'What shall
we do today?'

'Could we go to Disneyland?' Kit asked at once;
it was his favourite way of passing a day and it
was only an hour's drive away. Christie nodded.

'Why not?' At least it would keep her mind off
her own problems; she'd rather laugh over Mickey
Mouse than fret about the way Logan made her
feel. She was tired of her own inconsistencies; she
had been scared stiff of being alone in the house
with Logan while Kit was asleep, yet when Logan
obligingly cleared out and she could feel safe all
she had felt was jealous and angry. When she was
with Logan all they did was quarrel; she should be

delighted that he was otherwise occupied and wasn't bothering her.

When she and Kit returned that afternoon, though, Logan was back. She saw his car in the garage and Kit rushed off, yelling: 'Daddy! We're home!'

Christie locked her own car, frowning. She didn't like the way Kit had said that; it sounded too permanent. He mustn't start imagining that the way things were at the moment was the way they were always going to be in future; but as she followed slowly she couldn't think of a way of breaking it to him gently that she didn't intend to go on living with his father and she didn't mean him to stay there, either.

Logan and Kit were in the sitting-room watching television; Kit curled up on his father's lap with Logan's arm round him. Christie stood in the doorway, feeling unwanted and miserable, and Logan turned his head and looked at her, his grey eyes penetrating. She didn't want him to read her feelings; she turned and went out into the kitchen and began getting Kit's supper.

She heard him talking to his father, telling him what a great time they had had at Disneyland. Logan laughed occasionally, then she heard his deep voice talking warmly to Kit and Kit chuckling. Christie automatically spread peanut butter on Kit's thin sandwiches, got an apple and poured him some fresh orange juice from the fridge.

Kit ate supper, then ran back to his father, and Christie went upstairs to her own room to change. There were grass stains on her jeans and some ice-cream on the collar of her shirt where Kit had leaned against her while he ate an ice-cream cone, during one of the rides at Disneyland. She meant to get some steaks for dinner; she had bought some on their way back. She hadn't asked Logan if he would be going out, but he hadn't said he wouldn't be in for dinner, so presumably she would be cooking for two. She picked out a rose-pink silk dress which was very pretty but casual enough for an evening at home. Her reflection showed her a face which was far too tense and far too flushed. She glared at it, scowling. 'Oh, don't be such a fool,' she told herself, and went firmly out of the room to take Kit up to bed.

Logan was watching the early evening news. He kissed Kit and promised to come up and read a bedtime story in ten minutes. He didn't even look at Christie.

She left Kit in bed, waiting, and went down to remind Logan. 'Are you going out tonight?' she asked as he rose.

'No,' he said, calmly, and she backed into the kitchen like a nervous schoolgirl and immediately broke a plate as she got it out of the plate rack.

From the stairs Logan asked drily: 'Having fun?'

'Oh, go to hell,' Christie muttered as she got the dustpan and brush to sweep up the pieces. She washed her hands after she had tipped the remnants into the trash can, and began to prepare a meal. Logan came down and stood in the doorway, watching her.

'Don't hover,' she snapped. 'Either come in and help or go away. It's steak and salad, and if you don't like it . . .'

'I do,' he said, coming into the room. 'Broken any more of my crockery? Kit tells me you've already broken a glass today. It must be the novelty of doing domestic work; hardly your usual scene, I suppose.'

She turned on him, eyes flashing. 'I'm perfectly capable of running my own home. I'm a very good cook, as it happens.'

'When did you learn? You couldn't boil an egg when I was married to you.'

'That was years ago,' she said loftily. 'I've learnt a lot since then.'

His brows arched. 'How intriguing! Are you going to demonstrate all your newfound skills for me?'

Christie's face burned as she absorbed the double meaning in that remark, but she refused to rise to the bait. She had tossed a salad and made the dressing; now she slid the two pieces of fillet steak on to the grill, while Logan watched ironically.

'Shall I lay the table in the dining alcove?' she asked uncertainly. The dining-room was elegant and spacious; Christie felt they would be lost in it if there were just the two of them at the oval rosewood table. It was a room meant for big dinner parties; formal affairs with silver candelabra in the centre of the table and candlelight gleaming on polished wood and silver and crystal. 'Or the dining-room?'

'In here,' Logan murmured. 'More intimate.'

She turned away, trembling, to pick up the cutlery, and Logan suddenly caught her shoulders and spun her to face him. Knives and forks spilled to the floor with a loud clatter and she jumped, her nervous eyes flying to his face.

'Stop it, Christie!'

'Stop what?' she asked in a pretence of calm, but her voice quivered.

'All the drama,' he snapped. 'Don't shiver like that every time I come near you. What are you so scared of?'

'I'm not scared of anything,' she said with sweeping disregard of the truth, and saw Logan's hard mouth indent impatiently.

'Oh, yes—you are! Shall I tell you what scares you? Being a woman, a real, live, breathing, flesh and blood woman instead of a celluloid doll that no man can touch when she's safely up there on a screen. That's why you've been such a success in films. That's the only time you're really alive. It has to be make-believe fantasy love making for you, doesn't it? You can't take real passion. You might actually be expected to feel something instead of just mimicking emotion.'

Her colour flooded out of her face. White and angry, she stared back at him shaking her head. 'That's a lie—what a vile thing to say, it isn't true!'

'Isn't it?' He let go of her shoulders, but only to force his fingers into her hair, thrusting her head back. 'Show me,' he said huskily and as his mouth came down she gave a wild cry of protest, struggling to break free.

It was what she had both hungered for—and dreaded, she was torn in two directions at once; her mind fighting and ordering her body to resist, her body weakening rapidly as Logan's mouth took possession of hers and forced her lips to part.

A curious weakness and lassitude made her lean on him; she felt tired and wanted to cry. She kept reminding herself that nothing had changed; she refused to give up her career, it was too essential a part of her. Logan hadn't altered, either. If she gave in to him now the fights would start sooner or later, and this time she might get mauled beyond curing. She was older, less able to recover from the scars of love. Logan could hurt her more than any man she had ever met. Why should she give him the chance?

Her body was shaking as his hands caressed it; her lips surrendered to the insistent desire in his exploring mouth. Her mind was in turmoil. Logan undid her zip and she felt his hand sliding down her naked back. The rose pink silk crept lower and Logan's mouth pressed into her throat and then her bare, smooth shoulders. Christie's head fell back, a faint moan shaking her. Her hands went up to stroke his black hair as he kissed the deep valley between her breasts, and then she frowned, breaking out of that languor, her nostrils quivering.

'Oh, the steak,' she whispered. 'The steak's burning.'

Logan lifted his head. He was darkly flushed and breathing quickly. 'Damn the steak,' he muttered. He stretched out an arm and turned off the grill. Christie tried to wriggle out of his embrace and he caught her again, his hands relentless.

'Logan, I'm not going to bed with you!' she muttered, turning her head aside as his lips searched for hers again, and she heard him draw a harsh breath, his body going rigid.

'Oh, yes, you are, Christie. Tonight, you're mine. I'm tired of watching you on celluloid. I want the flesh and blood woman in my bed tonight, and I'm going to have you.' He picked her up while she kicked and hit out at him and walked out of the kitchen with her, one arm under her legs and the other under her back. 'Keep wriggling like that and I'll drop you,' he threatened. 'Right down these stairs!'

She lay back, deciding he might just do that, and watched the tough angles of his profile through lowered lids. Her temples were beating with blood and her throat had closed up in a mixture of panic and desire. Why not? she thought, shuddering. She wanted him, the very thought of making love with him was sending her crazy; she couldn't deny the deep, persistent ache inside her, why bother to try? She could go to bed with him tonight and walk out of here tomorrow—who was to stop her? Logan hadn't stopped her when she left him before.

Yet although she knew she could leave him in the morning, she was still afraid, because the very depth of her hunger for him told her that she wouldn't find it so easy to go. Once he had reminded her just what pleasure she got in his arms she wasn't going to be satisfied with just one night with him. Her body was already burning, her need for him was so intense it was physically painful.

Logan carried her into his bedroom and kicked the door shut with his foot before walking over to drop her on to the bed. She scrambled away from him and crouched on it, huddled like a child, her arms folded protectively across herself, in that timeless female gesture of self-defence.

'Logan, listen to me—you've never listened to me. Listen to me now. Please!'

'I've done all the talking I'm going to do tonight,' Logan muttered hoarsely, undoing his shirt, and Christie saw from his set face that she wasn't going to be able to talk calmly to him. She slid off the bed and darted to the door, while he was dropping his jacket and shirt on a chair. She heard Logan running behind her as she escaped from the room. Her own door stood open, she ran into it and slammed it shut, bolting it.

CHAPTER TEN

'OPEN it, Christie!' Logan called fiercely through the panels. 'Unless you want me to break it down!'

'You'll wake Kit,' she whispered.

She heard him swear. 'You can't stay in there for ever,' he said in a lower tone. 'Come out before I lose my temper.'

'I'm going to bed,' she said, and walked away. She was sure she heard him swearing again, but he was afraid to break down the door in case it woke Kit and upset him. He walked away and Christie sat down on her bed, almost in a state of collapse, her knees too weak to support her. She suddenly realised that her rose pink silk had been torn during her struggle with Logan. She pulled it over her head and dropped it into the laundry basket.

She couldn't hear any sound outside her door, Logan must have gone downstairs. The steaks would be ruined, he would have to eat salad for dinner, she thought irrelevantly, her eyes hot with unshed tears. She stripped and put on a thin white lawn nightdress, then climbed into her bed and lay there in the warm darkness, struggling with tears. Why did the one man she really wanted have to be the one man who was impossible? She turned her face into the pillow, sobbing. She had been trying to deny it to herself ever since they met again, but what was the point? She was still in love with him; she was crazy about him. He only had to look at her to send her temperature soaring. She would give anything to be in his bed right now.

Anything—except myself, she thought bitterly, and her self-respect and integrity was the price Logan demanded for the pleasure his body gave her, he wasn't satisfied with less than everything. He wanted her mind and soul as well as her body, and Christie refused to give him those essential elements of herself. Her heart he had had ever since she first saw him, when she was eighteen, but even at that age she had had a strong sense of the necessary dignity of the individual mind and will. Logan wanted to be the one who made all the decisions; the one who dominated and ruled. His masculinity insisted on it, and Christie's femininity had rebelled against such total submission. She wasn't going to abandon her sense of herself now.

The room was quiet and dark and her body ached with desire; frustration ate her as she turned on the pillow, the sheets were already hot where her body had lain, she felt her ears buzzing with the vibration of her blood and put her hands over them, tossing her head from side to side almost in a frenzy. She had left the windows wide open to let cooler night air circulate and the curtains blew softly against the carpet.

A sound startled her. She sat up, heart ramming against her breastbone, and saw a black shape in the room between her and the windblown curtain. Christie gave a terrified cry. The intruder launched himself across the room as she sat up in bed. His heavy body knocked her backwards, sprawling helplessly with him above her, his hand clamping over her mouth to stifle any more screams.

Above the hand her eyes stared at him as she tried to bite his fingers, and he whispered: 'I thought you didn't want to wake Kit?'

The mockery was a relief and at the same time maddening as she realised that it was Logan. 'How . . .' she mumbled against his hand, her body limp and bathed in sweat.

'I climbed from my balcony on to yours—your window was wide open. You shouldn't open the windows at night, it invites burglars. Use the air-conditioning if you're hot.' He looked at her wickedly, his eyes a gleam of silver in the darkness. 'Were you hot, Christie?'

She shuddered at the remorseless intrusion of his hand as it caressed her breast and slid down the curve of her body in the thin lawn nightdress. Logan was wearing a short towelling robe, it parted as he lay down beside her and she saw the ripple of muscle under his tanned skin. He lifted his hand from her mouth, but before she could say anything he was kissing her with insidious persuasion, his lips warm and sensitive, coaxing, teasing, demanding. His hand was inside the fragile barrier of the white lawn nightdress; it moved on her hot skin, tormenting her, and she turned her body into him, her arms round his neck, giving up in wordless surrender to her own desire. Logan shrugged out of the robe and Christie touched him, shaking, so aroused that she didn't know what she was saying or doing any more, her hot lips murmuring almost inaudibly.

Logan lifted her and stripped the nightdress from her without any resistance on her part now. He stared at her slight, naked body on the crumpled sheets and she groaned at the look in his eyes, holding out her arms to him.

'What did you say?' he whispered as he entered her, and she repeated dazedly, 'I want you.'

'No, before that,' he said huskily, touching her lips with the tip of his tongue.

'I love you,' she said, her arms round his back and her parted thighs holding him, and Logan kissed her deeply, fiercely, hurting her.

As he drove into her, her breathing quickened; her body moving in harmony with his in one rhythmic pulse, her head turning from side to side on the pillow, her lips parted in gasping breaths which sounded more like anguish than pleasure, so intense was the feeling inside her. She arched moaning, digging her nails into his back without knowing she was doing it, and Logan groaned a response, his mouth at her breast as though he was a child, the roughness of his hair brushing her bare skin. Christie could not halt the cries that broke from her a moment later. Logan half-laughed. 'Ssh . . . remember Kit!' and then he moved against her fiercely, merging with her and lying still as he almost sobbed with pleasure, his whole body pulsating.

She felt completely limp, sated, her skin drenched in perspiration and her body aching from his possession. Logan shifted and half lay beside her, half covered her, an arm across her and a leg tethering her to him. Christie closed her eyes with a long sigh. Logan's head was on her shoulder, she rested her chin on his hair and let herself slip into sleep.

When she woke up she was unable to remember

where she was for a second or two; then she felt
the warm flesh against her and the heavy weight of
Logan's arm on her. She cautiously opened her
eyes, remembering with a fierce pang, and as she
tentatively shifted Logan moved his head to look
up at her.

She went pink.

'Good morning,' he said softly. 'I've been
watching you while you slept; what long eyelashes
you've got. I thought they were false at first.'

Christie was too nervous to speak. She looked at
the window and saw that it was etched in grey; it
was just dawn and the sun wasn't yet up.

'It won't work,' she said, staring at the pale
outline of the window fixedly. 'I'm not giving up
my career, Logan. It means too much to me.'

'I won't ask you to give it up,' he told her, and
that surprised her into looking at him with
incredulous eyes.

'You won't ask me to? But you always wanted
me to stop work.'

'I was wrong,' he said, and that surprised her
even more, she couldn't believe her ears, and
Logan looked at her expression with a wry smile.
'I know, I'm not known for changing my mind,
but I have—I've done some thinking while I lay
here watching you sleep. I love you, Christie, I
loved you the minute I first saw you in London
when you were so young I should have had more
sense than to think of marrying you. It just
happened. I fell like a ton of bricks on sight and I
knew there would never be anyone else but you. I
was too old for you and too set in my thinking,
but I loved you, and I wouldn't let myself think

about the problems. I didn't think them out then, I swept them under the carpet and told myself that you'd soon come round to my way of thinking. That was arrogant and selfish of me. I blame myself for what came after that.'

'No,' she said with a sigh. 'I was partly to blame, too. I didn't think much, either. I knew I wanted to act and I knew I wanted you—it never occurred to me at first that there was any clash between the two things.'

'You were too young,' said Logan. 'Why should you have realised what I didn't even admit myself?'

'We never really talked, did we?' said Christie with sudden regret. If they had, would they ever have parted? Had she wasted five years of her life for nothing?

'I was too aware how young you were,' said Logan with a grimace, propping himself up on his elbow to look into her face. 'I tried to act like a father instead of a husband.'

Her eyes gleamed. 'I don't know about that—I didn't notice anything fatherly about you.'

He laughed huskily. 'Not in the bedroom, maybe. But out of it I tried to run your life for you, didn't I? The more we argued, the angrier I got. You wouldn't give way to me, and that made me so frustrated I lost my temper. I got to the point where I was ready to force you to do what I wanted.' He looked at her with a sort of sadness, his eyes dark. 'I'm sorry for that, Christie. I hated myself for it afterwards, but it was too late, you'd gone, and you wouldn't see me, even after Kit was born.'

'It broke me up,' she said unsteadily, remembering it herself. 'It was like . . .'

'Rape,' he said, his face grim. 'Go on—say it, it's true. I don't know how I lived with myself afterwards. I veered between being angry with myself and being angry with you. I was a psychological mess. I decided the only thing I could do was give you the divorce you wanted, let you keep Kit, stay out of your life. It was the only apology I could bring myself to give you. It wasn't until I read that story in the newspapers and saw your picture, those men mauling you, fighting over you—that I lost my temper again and came to find you. I pretended it was concern over Kit, but although that was part of it, it was jealousy, too. I nearly blew my skull when I saw that picture!'

She lifted a lazy hand and brushed his hair back from his face. 'I did notice you seemed pretty mad!' She laughed suddenly. 'And it was all so silly—I didn't even know the guy. Ziggy lost his temper, too, and that wasn't like him. Some creep tries to make a pass at me, the next thing I know is that Ziggy's punching a hole in his face—it was funny, really.'

'I didn't think so,' said Logan. 'I'd heard about Molyneaux from Kit, of course. I knew he was always seeing you. When I saw that picture of him I disliked him on sight and told myself it was because I didn't want him bringing up my son, but I had other reasons, too.' He bent and kissed her lightly. 'I'm glad you didn't take him seriously. He had me worried for a while.'

'Nobody takes Ziggy seriously—that's his problem. He's a lovely guy, he's sweet-tempered and charming and very good-looking, but . . .' She shrugged, her face regretful. 'Well, it's hard to say what it is that's missing, but . . .'

'I checked up on him a little,' Logan told her. 'Asked around about him, tried to get some idea what sort of guy he was—I wasn't very impressed. I didn't like his choice of friends or the way he lived. It wasn't just jealousy over you—I didn't think he was a suitable stepfather for Kit.'

'No,' she agreed. 'I worked that out for myself in the end. I was never in love with Ziggy, but I liked him and I thought Kit did and that they'd get on if I married Ziggy. Then I realised it wouldn't work. I think I hurt Ziggy and I wish I hadn't, but it was no good marrying him feeling the way I did; especially as I'd already been through one bad . . .' she broke off, looking at him uncertainly, and Logan grimaced.

'One bad marriage? That was what you were going to say, wasn't it? Yes, it was bad—for both of us, but it needn't have been, Christie. I married you without realising what marriage means. I thought I knew. I hadn't any doubts that what I wanted from our marriage was just how marriage should be—I was glad you were so young, I thought you'd be the sort of wife I wanted, I'd be able to train you into it. Maybe that's one reason I fell for you; I was probably looking for a young wife to train.' He looked at her with a bitter self-derision in his eyes. 'My God, I had a lot to learn. I thought I was going to teach you! And it was me that got taught. It wasn't until I'd lost you that I realised how much I needed you.' He put his head on her breasts, his body wrenched with a deep sigh. 'If you come back to me, it will be very different this time. I promise you, Christie. Don't leave me again.'

She put her cheek on his hair. 'You'll let me go on with my career?'

'Yes, you can do what you like. I'll never try to coerce you again.'

'I want to try some stage work. I might get a job in the local rep. if they'll have me—or I'll try some of the little theatres along the coast. I don't care if I have to take a walk-on at first. I want to learn my craft in a theatre before it's too late.'

Logan started to say something and there was a rapping at the door in the middle of his first sentence. He stopped, looking startled. 'Who the . . .'

Christie laughed. 'Kit,' she said. 'He wakes up early and wants his breakfast.' She stretched with a lazy smile. 'I did it yesterday—it's your turn today.'

Kit tapped again, louder.

'I get the feeling you're starting the way you mean to go on,' said Logan with a thoughtful look. 'Is that the way it's going to be? Turn and turn about?'

'Fifty-fifty,' Christie said lightly but meaning it. 'Whether it's Kit or cooking or doing the shopping. We'll need Janet, of course; she's wonderful with Kit and he loves her. While we're working we needn't worry about what's going on at home if Janet's here.'

'Mummy!' Kit called through the door. 'Mummy, Daddy's not in bed and his clothes are all over the floor!'

'His eyes are too sharp,' Logan said with a groan, swinging out of the bed and picking up his robe from the floor. 'I'm coming, Kit,' he called. 'Run on into the bathroom and wash and I'll make breakfast.'

There was a silence, then Kit's footsteps trotted back into his own room and Logan tied his belt while he looked at Christie with naked passion.

'I love you, did I tell you that?'

'Eloquently,' she said with a husky break in her voice. 'And I love you.' She paused, considering him through her lashes, her lips curving in a smile. 'Will you marry me, Mr Gray?'

'This is so sudden,' said Logan, laughing. 'Do I get time to think your proposal over?'

'Don't keep me in suspense for ever,' she said sweetly, eyeing him with mockery. 'Perhaps I should have gone down on my knees?'

Logan bent and kissed her laughing mouth. 'Now that's a marvellous idea—I think I'm going to like modern marriage—it's so full of surprises!'

Kit tapped again. 'Daddy?'

'Yes, Kit, I'm coming.' Logan opened the door. 'Hurry up, we're going to bring Mummy her breakfast in bed. You can squeeze the oranges while I make the toast and coffee.'

Christie lay back, stretching deliciously, and smiled as she watched the sunlight dancing in the room.

Take these 4 best-selling novels FREE

Yes! Four sophisticated, contemporary love stories by four world-famous authors of romance FREE, as your introduction to the Harlequin Presents subscription plan. Thrill to **Anne Mather**'s passionate story BORN OUT OF LOVE, set in the Caribbean.... Travel to darkest Africa in **Violet Winspear**'s TIME OF THE TEMPTRESS....Let **Charlotte Lamb** take you to the fascinating world of London's Fleet Street in MAN'S WORLD ....Discover beautiful Greece in **Sally Wentworth**'s moving romance SAY HELLO TO YESTERDAY.

The very finest in romance fiction

Join the millions of avid Harlequin readers all over the world who delight in the magic of a really exciting novel. EIGHT great NEW titles published EACH MONTH! Each month you will get to know exciting, interesting, true-to-life people .... You'll be swept to distant lands you've dreamed of visiting .... Intrigue, adventure, romance, and the destiny of many lives will thrill you through each Harlequin Presents novel.

Get all the latest books before they're sold out!

As a Harlequin subscriber you actually receive your personal copies of the latest Presents novels immediately after they come off the press, so you're sure of getting all 8 each month.

Cancel your subscription whenever you wish!

You don't have to buy any minimum number of books. Whenever you decide to stop your subscription just let us know and we'll cancel all further shipments.